PRAISE

A Sure C~~ure for~~ ~~Witchcraft~~

"Filled with amazing characters, *A Sure Cure for Witchcraft* is an interesting and exciting story which spans centuries, opens up a historical era for young readers and well deserves a place in schools and libraries across the country."

–CM Reviews

"A beautifully written and thrilling adventure about friendship.... Middle-grade readers will gobble up this page-turner. Thought-provoking and inspiring, this book is sure to spark many conversations about women's empowerment!"

–Wendy McLeod MacKnight, author of *The Frame-Up*

"A beautifully written and evocative tale."

–Julie Lawson, author of *A Blinding Light*

"A well-researched work of historical fiction that will resonate today because of its focus on the power of healing."

–Atlantic Books Today

The Family Way

"This prequel to Laura Best's two previous novels about Cammie is another magnificent example of middle-grade historical fiction that truly resonates with readers of all ages."

–Canadian Children's Book News

"Tulia is a wonderful main character, an intriguing combination of adult and child....By the end of the novel, she is older, wiser, and infinitely more aware of the circumstances and events around her. Best makes the history come alive."

–Canadian Review of Materials, highly recommended

This is it,
LARK
HARNISH

Laura Best

This is it,
LARK
HARNISH

Laura Best

NIMBUS
PUBLISHING LTD.

Nimbus Publishing Limited
3660 Strawberry Hill Street, Halifax, NS, B3K 5A9
(902) 455-4286 nimbus.ca

Printed and bound in Canada
NB1443

Editor: Penelope Jackson
Editor for the press: Whitney Moran
Design: Jenn Embree
Typesetting: Rudi Tusek

Library and Archives Canada Cataloguing in Publication

Title: This is it, Lark Harnish / Laura Best.
Names: Best, Laura (Laura A.), author.
Identifiers: Canadiana (print) 20220235872 | Canadiana (ebook) 20220235880 |
ISBN 9781774711064 (softcover) | ISBN 9781774711071 (EPUB)
Classification: LCC PS8603.E777 T55 2022 | DDC jC813/.6—dc23

Nimbus Publishing acknowledges the financial support for its publishing activities from the Government of Canada, the Canada Council for the Arts, and from the Province of Nova Scotia. We are pleased to work in partnership with the Province of Nova Scotia to develop and promote our creative industries for the benefit of all Nova Scotians.

For my friend Oran
1907–2008

CHAPTER ONE

BELLA CLIP-CLOPPED UP THE LONG DRIVEWAY TO THE MCMASTER HOME-stead. For the first time that morning, I felt a queasiness in my stomach. Mama had been right: Brock Cameron was the perfect travelling companion. He'd entertained me with his stories all the way from Crawfordville. But the time for storytelling was over. I gripped my bag. Brock pulled on the reins and let out a soft "Whoa." Bella slowly came to a stop and Brock stepped down from the buggy. I drew in a deep breath; there was no turning back.

"This is it, little miss," Brock said, holding out his hand to steady me as I climbed out of his buggy. "Welcome to Upper Springdale. Now, right up to the front door with you. That's where Mrs. McMaster said to bring you."

Grabbing my bag of belongings, I hurried to keep up with Brock. "Goodbye, Bella," I called out. Bella raised her head and snorted.

Brock opened the front door and stepped aside for me to enter. I hesitated for a moment.

"Just walk right in. Mrs. McMaster will be along soon. I'll let her know you're here."

I smiled and pulled my bag close. Sooner or later I'd have to make a move. Brock slung the bag of parcels and letters over his shoulder and walked down the hallway.

"Thank you kindly for the ride," I called out cheerily. I couldn't help but smile. Brock Cameron put me in mind of Santa Claus toting his sack of toys—the tallest, skinniest Santa in the whole wide world.

Muffled voices came from somewhere inside the house. I looked all around me. A finer house I'd never seen. A gold-gilded mirror hung on the wall. I went to take a closer look but stopped. If I didn't look at all presentable, I didn't want to know. First impressions are important. Now was not the time to discover I looked a complete mess, and given the distance we'd travelled I most certainly did. I reached for any loose strands of hair the wind might have tugged free but to my relief felt none. There was little else I could do but smooth the wrinkles from my dress and wait for Mrs. McMaster.

Down the hallway, a door was slightly ajar. Sunbeams streamed through the opening and stretched out across the floor. What was inside that room—in all the rooms? Were they cluttered with knickknacks that would need constant dusting? Curiosity started a stampede of questions charging through me. Was Mrs. McMaster real fussy when it came to cleaning? Would my work suit her? Would she even like me? Movement to my left soon told me I wasn't the only one who was curious. Beside the staircase, a boy was inspecting me from head to toe. His dark brown hair was parted on the left and so neatly combed it looked as though someone might have taken a sadiron to it. I thought of my brother Frank, whose hair would go for days without seeing a comb if Mama was too busy to notice.

"Good day to you, young lad," I said, offering him my friendliest how-do-you-do smile. "What would your name be?"

He didn't answer but stood looking at me strangely. I wondered suddenly if I didn't look a fright after all. But I'm not one to give up easily. I wanted him to know there was no reason to be shy around me. It simply wouldn't do if we were to be in the same house together.

"Now, you must have a name. Everyone I know has a name, so don't go telling me you don't," I said with a smile. His eyes rolled in his head and he looked quite innocent standing there with his hands clasped in front of him. "What's the matter, cat got your tongue?" When a small grin touched his lips, I figured I didn't look so bad after all. But small grin or not, he still refused to speak. I tried another approach.

"I see you're a shy one, mister young lad. Perhaps you don't have a name at all. Imagine that, a boy without a name!"

Still my words had no effect, but that just made me more determined. There had to be some way to get him to speak.

"On second thought, you must have a name. Now, let me think," I said, tapping my finger thoughtfully against my cheek. "If I had to guess, I might say you look like an Egbert or a Montgomery."

His eyes bugged out and he quickly shook his head.

"No? Hmmm. I knew a young lad named Rosie once. Your name wouldn't be Rosie, would it? Short for Roosevelt, of course..." Again, he shook his head. "No? You're sure it's not Rosie? Let me see. How about Joe? I bet that's it!"

He made a small noise that sounded about halfway between a grunt and a giggle. I was finally getting to him with my silly talk. If I found the right words, I knew he'd speak. His shyness was as good as gone.

"What about Cortland, then? Not the apple, mind you. If you were an apple, I'd be making a pie out of you as we speak."

Finally, he let out a nervous giggle and I laughed along with him. Papa used to say that having a good laugh was a great way to start a friendship. Hopefully, I'd made my first friend. Things could only get better from here...or so I thought.

CHAPTER TWO

"**D**ID YOU FORGET WHAT PAPA TOLD US?" CAME A VOICE FROM ABOVE ME. The young lad and I both jumped. I looked up to see a girl at the top of the staircase, her hand resting on the railing. Her looks put me in mind of the porcelain doll Mrs. Hobbs has on the mantel in her parlour, the one her son brought all the way home from England after the war. Soft, dark curls dangled loosely about her face as she hurried down the steps, her gaze centred on the boy. Excited to make another friend, I waited for her to return my very best smile.

"You're not to be pestering the hired girl, Georgie," she said when she reached the bottom of the staircase with her nose curled upward. "You know what Grandmother told you."

"Georgie! See, I knew you had a name!" I burst out. The girl snapped her head around in my direction. She was scowling like a baby suffering from a bad case of colic. I saw then how wrong I had been. She didn't look the least bit like Mrs. Hobbs's doll. Diana has eyes that sparkle, a smiling mouth, and dimpled cheeks. And I just know she'd have a soft friendly voice if ever she was able to speak. This girl had the same dark curls as Diana, but that was where the resemblance ended.

"Never you mind, Sylvie," said another girl marching our way. Georgie scurried toward her and grabbed her hand. "Grandmother says he mustn't go making himself a nuisance. She didn't say he wasn't to smile...You're too bossy, Sylvie." She turned toward me. "I'm Martha," she said, smiling real big. Finally! Someone who wasn't afraid to smile.

"It's nice to meet you, Martha," I said politely, relieved to see a friendly smile aimed at me.

Martha didn't have the same curly hair as her sister. It was fashioned into two flawless braids. Two small pink bows held them in place and matched the dress she was wearing quite nicely.

"Papa said we were getting a hired girl to help Grandmother out," said Martha, turning back toward me. "He says she's busier than most people what with running the post office these days. It's terribly exciting...all those letters and parcels being delivered right here in our very own house. Like Christmas coming every Tuesday and Friday. I bet Rebecca O'Reily is being gobbled up with envy. She thinks she's so smart because her father owns the sawmill and most of the folks around here work for him. One day she told Michael Schaffer if it wasn't for her father he wouldn't be worth the bread and molasses he brought to school in his lunch kettle. Just wait till she comes someday to collect the mail. I'd love to be a fly on the wall when Grandmother hands it to her." Martha's smile turned to a scowl. "Only we're not allowed to go in there." She let out an airy sigh. "Grandmother says the post office is off limits to us children."

"Oh dear, how dreadfully dreadful." I couldn't imagine what it would feel like to have a room in your home that you were never allow to enter.

"Grandmother's so afraid a letter will get lost one day and she'll be the one to blame," said Martha.

"Martha only has to look at something and it disappears." Sylvie glared at her younger sister.

Martha whipped around to face her. "You're making that up, Sylvie, and you know what Grandmother says about *that*." I'm sure a cross-eyed bull couldn't have made a homelier face than Martha just then. I wanted to laugh but didn't dare.

"Do you want your face to get stuck that way?" Sylvie said in an uppity tone. Neither girl looked as though they were going to back down. I quickly tried to distract them before a tussle broke out.

"I wouldn't think a little peek inside the post office could hurt," I said in my cheeriest voice. "Why, a peek scarcely counts. In fact, it amounts to about the same as a speck, and no one even sees a speck."

"I suppose so," said Martha doubtfully as she turned back toward me. "Grandmother does take her job most seriously."

"And I should think. The job of postmistress is something to be taken quite seriously."

"Oh, *you'll* see, Grandmother takes everything seriously," said Sylvie with a smirk.

The smile returned quickly to Martha's face. "It might be nice to receive a letter. I wish someone would send me one."

"No one in their right mind would bother to post you a letter." Sylvie gave her sister a look of annoyance and stomped off through the house, calling for her grandmother.

"She's just mad because she's best friends with Rebecca, the snob. No one dares say anything about Rebecca in front of

Sylvie. When she comes to the house, she won't even talk to me...
Rebecca's perfect."

"Oh my, how utterly horrible! Imagine having to live up to
that reputation, not to mention how boring it would be. Mistakes
only make life interesting and give us a story to tell and, hopefully, something to laugh about later."

Just then Georgie stepped out from behind Martha. He was
staring at me as if I was from a foreign land.

"My name is Lark," I offered in my friendliest voice.

"Lark, that's a bird, isn't it?" asked Martha.

"Indeed it is. Papa named me. He said my singing would put
the birds to shame."

"Can you sing?" asked Martha hopefully.

"Not a note." I quickly smiled and added, "But it doesn't stop
me from trying. Music was important to Papa. He could play
most any instrument. Fiddle, harmonica—anything he set his
mind to."

Martha's face lit up. "Maybe someday he can come and play
our piano. Grandmother says it's just gathering dust in the parlour, and it's a darn shame that none of us has any musical talent.
Grandmother says she has a tin ear—whatever that is."

I didn't have time to explain that Papa would never be able
to play their piano.

Footsteps in the distance sounded like the clip-clopping of
Brock Cameron's horse. Martha grabbed her brother's hand and
scampered off. A forceful *ahem* vibrated in the air. Head high, a
woman was heading my way with Sylvie at her heels. Her shoes
continued to clack noisily against the hardwood floor. Surely this
was Mrs. McMaster. The time had come for me to make my good
impression. My stomach made a quick lurch. As the expanse

between us became smaller and the clacking of her shoes echoed louder, my heart sank slowly to the floor.

Mrs. McMaster wasn't at all what I was expecting. Not one bit.

CHAPTER THREE

MRS. MCMASTER LOOKED ME OVER AS THOUGH I HAD CREAM STUCK TO the corners of my mouth. She was a tall, sturdy woman. It was easy to see that her size alone would be enough to cause those around her to stand up and take notice. Her braided hair was amassed into a streaked grey bun on the top of her head. And the faint scent of lilacs was in the air. I was reminded of Mrs. Hobbs back home, the wonderfully sweet perfume that always followed her about.

"Lark Harnish, I would suspect?" And just the way Mrs. McMaster said it gave me the feeling that she thought I had done something wrong. Not "Glad to make your acquaintance" or "I hope you had a fine journey." Suspect? Suspect me of what? I wanted to cry. "How old did you say you were?"

"Thirteen," I squeaked, unable to think of anything else to add. I gave a weak smile and shifted awkwardly. I should have said I was fourteen, and I should have said it with my head held high. Fourteen sounds better, and really what difference would a year make? Nothing so far as I could see, except maybe put Mrs. McMaster's mind to rest. My work would speak for itself.

"I was told you were thirteen," she said, nodding stiffly.

Relief trickled through me. It was a test, and I'd passed. My honesty had paid off…So far, so good.

"But I daresay you're not very big." She let out a sigh, her nose curled up slightly as she continued her inspection of me. "I usually let my instincts guide me in these situations."

"I'm more than capable, Mrs. McMaster. I promise I am. Why, Mama—"

Her hand went up and she cut me off. "Quiet," she said, her face hard as stone. "There's a time to listen and a time to jabber. This is the time to listen."

I knew it! She wasn't at all pleased by the sight of me. I was too plain and simple; nothing special at all. My light brown hair was tied fast behind me. Perhaps I should have asked Mama to do something fancy with it. I caught a quick glimpse of Sylvie's beautiful blue dress as she stood behind her grandmother. I was suddenly conscious of the dress I'd started out with that morning. It was ordinary and yellow, dyed with onion skins. Mama made it special for today. She called it a workaday dress—practical and strong.

"It'll survive a hundred washings," she'd said last evening when she surprised me with it. As I pulled it down over my head this morning, I thought it was the best dress ever. Now I wasn't so sure. What if Mrs. McMaster had been expecting someone all prettied up like Martha and Sylvie? I stood motionless with my mouth shut, listening as she had instructed me to. I needed this job so badly I'd turn cartwheels if it would make her happy. Mrs. McMaster circled me like a hen hawk in the dooryard. Sylvie was smirking. When next Mrs. McMaster spoke, her mouth was ill-shaped, as though she'd just eaten something detestable.

"I'm not sure what I was expecting, Lark Harnish." I knew right then my first impression just went flying out the window. Still, I was determined not to become discouraged. This job was far too important. I'd have to come up with a way to win her over—and soon. But how would I do that if I wasn't allowed to speak?

"I daresay this could prove to be a disastrous venture for us both." She paused and I held my breath.

"Or a totally delightful one?" I said hopefully.

Her gaze settled on me again. Viewing the bothered look on her face, I cringed. This was still not going well, not at all.

"I suppose since you're here you might as well get started," she stated with a fair bit of reluctance. "I hope you know your way around a kitchen."

"Oh yes, Mrs. McMaster," I said with all the enthusiasm I could muster.

"Brock Cameron spoke quite highly of you. I hope you won't disappoint him—or me." She paused. "I'll give you a three-week trial, Lark Harnish. Two is generally expected these days. I daresay that's more than fair. Three weeks should tell the tale."

My heart made a happy flutter. Three weeks—things were definitely looking up! Three whole weeks to prove I was a good worker, someone who could be depended upon. I couldn't believe my good fortune.

I wanted to let out a shriek, at least thank her a million times over. I wanted to shout from the rooftop, but decided it was in my best interest to keep listening and not speak, at least for now. I pulled out an eager smile and waited for her to return one of her own. Her lips remained firm, but I was determined to believe that she wasn't nearly as surly as she let on. There was a sense of humour lurking somewhere inside everyone; Mrs. McMaster would be no different. I'd find it sometime during the next three weeks. No one could be grumpy all the time. And Brock, I'd thank Brock Cameron next time I saw him. I'm sure she wouldn't have agreed to this trial period at all if it wasn't for him.

"I haven't the time right now to show you about properly, what with the mail needing to be sorted and people soon coming. Sylvie will get you settled in your room." She turned toward Sylvie, all stiff and proper. "Set her to work in the kitchen when she's ready. There are plenty of dishes to be scoured. The kettle's humming as we speak. Do try and move quickly."

"Yes, Grandmother." Sylvie was still wearing the same smirk she'd sported earlier.

I needed to thank Mrs. McMaster before she left. It only seemed right that I express my gratitude for her giving me a chance. Reverend Bradley says it's important to give thanks in all circumstances. The time for me to talk was now.

"Thank you, Mrs. McMaster. Thank you from the very bottom of my overbrimming heart. And just so you know, it won't take me but a few moments to put what little I have away," I called out as she started down the hallway. I couldn't let her walk away, me standing there with my mouth clamped tight as an oyster's shell, if I expected to win her over. If I planned to get into her good graces, I had to start right away. Three weeks' pay wouldn't be much help to Mama, not even to get the grocery bill paid off. Opportunities like this don't just come along any old day of the week.

"Mama never allows us to dawdle, not when there's work to be done," I added quickly.

Mrs. McMaster turned back toward me and the oddest expression crossed her face. Good or bad, I had her attention. I smiled.

"And yes, my name really is Lark Harnish, in case you suspected you weren't talking to the right person. Brock Cameron brought me here this morning—along with the mail. You won't be sorry for this, Mrs. McMaster. I promise, you won't."

Mrs. McMaster let out a grunt. "That remains to be seen," she said with a steady jaw. "Now, I haven't time for all your gibberish. Just get yourself settled in."

As she turned and marched away, she released a sound of utter annoyance. I wanted to shrink into oblivion. What could I have been thinking, letting my tongue waggle on so? If I planned to impress Mrs. McMaster, I was doing a pretty shabby job of it. I took a big breath and grabbed my bag up off the floor. These next weeks could prove to be very challenging indeed.

Chapter Four

"FOLLOW ME. YOUR ROOM IS AT THE TOP OF THE STAIRS—THREE DOORS down. There's another set of steps. Grandmother said you're to use them," said Sylvie with her nose turned toward the ceiling. She had the same prissy sound in her voice earlier when she was scolding her brother. We marched up the stairs, and when we reached the top, Georgie and Martha joined the procession.

"We call it the little room," added Martha as we waddled behind Sylvie like a brood of baby ducks. Little or not, it would be a room of my own, with a bed all to myself.

"The little room sounds totally delightful," I said with the fake British accent I use when Midge and I play a game we called Buckingham Palace. I wanted to laugh—as if Queen Mary would ever have a reason to speak about a "little room." Buckingham Place would have chambers—much more elegant.

Martha and Georgie giggled at my silly talk. Sylvie stopped abruptly. She spun around and gave us a look that could have stopped a crow mid-flight. I snapped my head front and centre, then looked over at Martha and grinned. Silence was expected while Sylvie gave me the grand tour.

"You won't need a whole lot of room," continued Sylvie. "Grandmother says you won't be spending much time there anyway. It'll be plenty warm in the winter."

The hallway was long. I wondered if I would remember how to get back to my room come nighttime. A portrait of a woman on the wall stopped me in my tracks. I studied her beautiful face. Her smile was delicate and she had the most pleasant look.

"That's our mother," said Martha when she saw me looking at the photo. She reached out and touched the frame. "Isn't she lovely?"

"Indeed," I whispered. She stood poised in a long, flowing dress. I could scarcely imagine standing that still, not even long enough to have my picture taken.

"She's gone," said Martha. "I can't even remember her. Sylvie does. Don't you, Sylvie?"

"What difference does it make what I remember?" snapped Sylvie. "Grandmother says it's wrong to hang on to the past, and we shouldn't go wishing for people to come back from the dead." She turned quickly and marched on ahead.

"Sylvie's being mean today," whispered Martha. "She didn't want Grandmother to get a hired girl."

"Oh dear." No wonder she seemed so bad-tempered.

"Sylvie doesn't like strangers. She just got used to Trent and Firth being around, and they've been here nearly six months. They work for Papa with the horses. Do you like horses, Lark?"

"Papa used to say that anyone worth their salt likes horses."

Martha frowned. "You mustn't say that around Grandmother. She says she's hardly fond of the 'wretched beasts,' even though we'd be lost without them. She says they smell."

"Of course they smell—that's why they have noses!"

Sylvie cleared her throat. "Are you coming, Lark?" she called out. "Grandmother *did* say to hurry."

Looking over at Martha and George, I grinned, then hurried to catch up to Sylvie. I'd never been scolded so many times in one day, and by someone younger than myself. But I wasn't about to let that discourage me. I had a job. I'd make friends with Sylvie one way or another. If I could convince Mrs. McMaster to keep me on after my three-week trial, surely making friends with Sylvie would be possible too.

CHAPTER FIVE

"GRANDMOTHER SAYS YOU'RE TO KEEP THINGS TIDY."

The room might have been small by the McMasters' standards, but it was plenty big for me, seeing how I was used to sharing a room with Midge. The flowered paper on the walls, pretty pink-and-yellow blossoms with green leaves, reminded me of Mama's flowerbed. For a moment I imagined myself picking a bright bouquet for Mrs. McMaster. I was sure it had been a long time since someone had surprised *her* with flowers. I'd present them to her and stand back while she fell all over herself, thanking me for being so thoughtful. Maybe she'd even apologize for not being able to scare up a small pinch of friendliness when she greeted me earlier. When Martha and Georgie climbed onto the bed, I snapped out of my daydream. Mrs. McMaster wouldn't care about some imaginary flowers, even if they were for her.

My entire bag took little time to unpack. Everything fit in one drawer: four pairs of stockings, undergarments, three dresses Mama had made from flour sacks, a hairbrush, and two gowns for sleeping in. Sylvie and Martha were wearing store-bought dresses. I couldn't imagine Mrs. McMaster ever sewing a dress from flour sacks for them. I wondered then what it must be like to be one of the McMaster children, never wanting for anything so far as I could see.

At the bottom of my bag was a box of stationery with pretty pink roses at the top, a writing pen, and a bottle of ink. It was a going-away gift from Mrs. Hobbs.

"You'll want to write home, of course," she'd said the day she gave it to me. Mama had smiled and said it was far too generous a gift.

"I daresay we'll all want to hear about Lark's adventures," Mrs. Hobbs said, patting Mama's hand.

I placed the writing supplies on top of the nightstand. I could hardly wait to write Mama.

"There," I said when everything was put away. "I told you it wouldn't take long." Sylvie quickly turned away. Off we headed again with Sylvie in the lead.

The kitchen certainly had its share of dirty dishes, stacked neatly on the table. "You're to use those tea towels," she said, pointing to the line above the wood stove. "Grandmother wants them washed each time. Grandmother can't abide a dingy tea towel. The dishpan's on the table next to the dishes, and there's plenty of water in the kettle and a bucket of cold water in the porch."

"Can we stay and watch you work?" asked Martha.

"I don't see why not. It'll help make the time go faster if I have company. I'm used to having folks around me most of the time. Midge, my younger sister, why, she's practically my shadow."

"Grandmother said we were not to be bothering you," said Sylvie, firmly.

"Oh, it's no bother at all. I'm sure we'd have fun. You'd be doing me a favour."

"Grandmother *is* the one in charge," insisted Sylvie. "I don't think she'd like for the hired girl to be telling us what to do. Come on, Georgie and Martha."

As they went on their way, I let out a sigh. It might have been nice to have someone to talk to, seeing how I'd only just arrived and everything was all so very new. What if I had questions? Or couldn't find something? I rolled up my sleeves and went for the kettle.

With my hands settled in the dishwater, I considered my current situation. When Brock Cameron told me that Mrs. McMaster was in need of a helping hand, I couldn't decide whether to take the job or not. Mama was so against it.

"You're just a girl, Lark," she'd said. "You should be learning your lessons and having fun, not cooking and cleaning for strangers."

Then Cooper spoke up and said it was my decision and no one else's.

"But I don't know how to decide," I said, looking from Mama to Cooper.

"Sometimes, you have to look inside and ask yourself the right questions," said Cooper. "And when you ask the right questions, it only makes sense that you'll get the right answers." It sounded like something Papa would have said. I guess Mama thought so too. She reluctantly said she'd leave it up to me.

I gave Cooper's suggestion a try. I looked all around the house, in every nook and cranny. I examined the room where Midge and I slept, the quilt stretched out across the bed, the Star of Annapolis Royal. Mama made it when she was about my age. I thought about Midge and me running barefoot across the cold floors on winter mornings, and the times we crawled beneath the quilts to get dressed, so cold we could see our breath, and how good the warmth from the wood stove felt as we crawled down from the loft.

I thought about waking to the sounds of songbirds sitting in the tree outside our bedroom window in the springtime and the cluck-clucking of the chickens in the dooryard as they scratched in the dirt for bugs.

I looked at Mama's good apron hanging on the wall in the kitchen. I imagined her coming across the field, her apron filled with red apples, and Mama in the kitchen paring off the skins for making pies.

I walked past the places I wouldn't see for a long time if I left Crawfordville. I peeked in through the windows of the school-house. Would I find it unbearable not to be learning things from books? Papa never went to school a day in his life and he got along just fine. Having had seven years of schooling, I was better off than Papa in that respect. Book-learning is important, but so are other things; like being someone people can count on, someone who tells the truth and helps others out when they need it, someone who has a good heart even if they jabber too much. I wouldn't mind leaving school behind.

Mrs. Hobbs once told Mama that the best a girl can hope for is to marry well and raise a family. Mama was plenty annoyed when she told Mrs. Hobbs there was more a girl can do besides raise a family.

"I suppose there's nursing or teaching," Mrs. Hobbs said.

"Or carpentry or doctoring. Maybe even banking," Mama added, snapping her head as she spoke. Mrs. Hobbs let out a snort.

"Never settle for things just because folks think you should," Mama told me later. "You can do whatever you set your mind to. Don't be afraid to dream big, Lark."

More important than the things I would miss if I left Crawfordville was the reason for me to go in the first place. The influenza took Papa from us after the war was over. Folks said it killed more people than the war. With Papa gone there was no room for me to be a child anymore, to play games and squander away my days, to dream the big dreams Mama talked about. It was only right that I make my own way. Every month I'd watch Mama take a small amount of money and give it to Mr. Hubley, the grocer. I saw the look on her face when he'd tell her how much was still owed on the bill.

"Don't you worry, Jane," Mr. Hubley said one day. "Everyone needs a helping hand from time to time."

"Ray never believed in owing for anything," Mama said, shaking her head.

"And a poor neighbour and friend I'd be not to help out at a time like this," Mr. Hubley said with a gentle smile. I knew it pained Mama to be in his debt, but without Mr. Hubley we'd have been facing a real calamity. Sometimes Mama would trade fresh eggs or cream for the things we needed. Mr. Hubley was more than happy to get them.

"You can sure tell these eggs are laid by contented hens," he'd say.

"What's a contented hen?" Frank asked one day.

"A contented hen means a happy hen," Mama explained.

"I never saw a hen smile before," said Frank, scratching his head. All Mama and I could do was laugh.

Mama could use the money I'd make working for the McMasters. I was determined to help pay off that grocery bill, no matter how long it took. I didn't want Mama to worry. Cooper was working as an apprentice in Mr. Nichols's blacksmith shop, but starting wages were low. Even though Mrs. McMaster didn't seem very friendly, I had to make the best of it for Mama's sake. I had to do everything to Mrs. McMaster's satisfaction and then some. I had to make sure she kept me on when my three weeks were up. One way or another, I'd make her glad to have hired me.

Chapter Six

"MAKE SURE TO USE SOME ELBOW GREASE, LARK; THAT HALLWAY FLOOR mortifies me the way it shows the dirt."

"Yes, Mrs. McMaster, elbow grease for sure," I said, bearing down harder with the scrub brush in my hand. Ignoring the hurt in both my knees, I was determined to do my very best.

Mrs. McMaster had been hovering over me ever since the day's mail had been sorted, inspecting each thing I did. The weight of her scrutiny was on my back. It was not the best circumstances for working under, especially on my very first day, but I'd have to get used to it.

"A clean floor says just one thing: the entire house is clean. The second I walk into a house I can tell what kind of people live there. Cleanliness *is* next to godliness, they say."

What would our floors back home tell Mrs. McMaster about us? Frank was forever tracking in mud. Midge wasn't a whole lot better. And what about the day Frank left the back door open and Clementine strolled right into the kitchen, clucking and scratching? When Mama found her perched on the arm of the rocking chair, the feathers went flying. I could almost bet if Mrs. McMaster had come to our house any one of those times, she wouldn't have offered me a three-week trial; she wouldn't have offered a trial period at all. She would have curled her nose up and refused to let me in her house. Dipping the scrub bush into the bucket, I started scrubbing another spot on the floor. I rubbed hard, thinking that what Mrs. McMaster didn't know surely wouldn't make her feel the least bit mortified.

"You should have seen the hands on that Parker boy today," she said as I moved my bucket down the hallway. "Why, I almost fell over when he came to pick up the mail for his mother. Why must children get themselves so filthy?"

"To keep their parents busy making soap, I suspect."

"Seems to me if they were the ones having to make the soap, they might think twice. I could only look at that child with regret," she shuddered.

I let out a small giggle as I pushed the scrub brush back and forth the floor.

"I hardly think it's amusing, Lark Harnish."

"No, ma'am," I said, scrubbing a little harder.

"Oh, bother!" exclaimed Mrs. McMaster later that afternoon. "Here come the men in from the hayfield and supper isn't on the table. Where did the afternoon fly to? Well, they'll just have to wait. That's all that's to it."

From the kitchen window, I saw a fine team of horses being led into the barn. I was reminded of Jim, Papa's beautiful dapple-grey horse and the tinkling of the harness bells in the frosty winter air, the way Jim would lift his head and tail when he trotted down the road. Papa would get that certain twinkle in his eye after a fall of fresh snow.

"Let's hitch up the sleigh. It's time we had a little fun," he'd say, stirring us with excitement.

"Don't stand there looking off into thin air, Lark Harnish! I dare say there's plenty for you to do without you standing around like you're on holiday."

"Yes, Mrs. McMaster," I said, snapping out of my reverie. If only I'd had a few more moments to dream. It was always that way. Whenever I found a sweet memory of Papa, something always yanked it away from me.

"I knew this day was doomed to go backwards," Mrs. McMaster started in. "The floors—you spent far too much time on the floors, Lark. You'll have to learn to do your chores more quickly. Then again, I wasn't much help myself, and your very first day at that. Perhaps it wasn't such a good idea having you come on mail day." She sighed, pulling a stray lock of hair off her forehead. "Come along now, the carrots need butter and the potatoes still have to be drained."

Hurrying to do what Mrs. McMaster asked, I went for the pot of potatoes.

"On second thought, set the table. I'll drain the potatoes. The plates and cutlery—Sylvie, show Lark where they are and then go fetch Martha and George."

Scurrying around like a field mouse, I tried hard to stay out of Mrs. McMaster's way.

Right…left…left…right, my mind puzzled over which side of the plate the forks went on. I couldn't ask for help with something so simple. I glanced up to see Sylvie standing in the doorway watching me. She turned away and I finally made my decision. Left—the forks go on the left. When Mrs. McMaster didn't correct me, I knew I'd made the right choice.

Mrs. McMaster made a quick survey of the kitchen, checking to make sure everything was perfect. "I believe we did it, Lark." Finally, she sounded pleased about something. "We'll put supper on the table as soon as the men sit down. Go outside and call them in."

I stood between the house and barn and called out a hearty "Supper's ready!" A man appeared in the doorway of the barn. I recognized him as one of the men who had helped bring the team of horses in earlier.

"Good day to you, miss," he called out, lifting his hat in a gentlemanly way. "You must be the hired girl Mrs. McMaster spoke of. Come all the way from Crawfordville, I hear."

"Yes indeed. I'm Lark Harnish."

"Trent Gates, here. Pleased to make your acquaintance." Another man emerged from the barn and stood beside him. Trent nodded at him and said, "This here's my brother, Firth. Watch out for him. He's a mean one, Miss Lark. Too mean for his own good, he is. Even too mean to grow hair."

He pulled his brother's hat off. To my surprise there was barely a stray hair to be seen on the top of his head. There were two small tufts of hair right next to his ears, yet the top was a bald as a baby's backside. Firth didn't change his expression as Trent set the hat back on his brother's head. I couldn't stop laughing, for Firth remained as solemn as a minister at a funeral and Trent was as cheery as they come. The two of them made the funniest sight. They headed toward the back door, and once the giggles were out of me, I called out to Trent, "I believe you're lucky to have such a good-natured brother."

"He's even too mean to waste a smile." Trent playfully nudged Firth with his elbow as they walked along.

I hurried toward the house, feeling carefree for the first time that day. How good it felt to share a laugh, to feel that someone here might actually like me.

But then Mrs. McMaster appeared in the doorway, and she did not look the least bit pleased.

"Now is not the time for fun and games, Lark Harnish. Supper is getting cold."

My heart made a mad leap and I sucked in a big breath. Mrs. McMaster stepped out onto the doorstep to allow Trent and Firth inside.

"I would think you'd be on your way to getting cleaned up by now," she said to them. "You are holding up supper."

"For sure, Mrs. McMaster," said Trent. "We were having us a time unhitching the team. They get their contrary spells, they do. And if I didn't know better, I'd have to say they must have got up on the wrong side of the bed this morning."

"Wrong side of the bed," snorted Mrs. McMaster. "Have your fun, Trent Gates, but life is not a field day." By this time, she was wagging her finger at him. "It's serious business. We can't spend our days acting the clown."

As she turned back toward the doorway, I struggled to hold in the giggle bubbling up inside me. I wasn't at all sure I'd be able to take life as serious as Mrs. McMaster wanted me to.

"Has everyone washed up?" asked Mrs. McMaster once we were all situated in the kitchen. Sylvie and Martha lined up in front of their grandmother. They stuck out their palms and Mrs. McMaster carefully inspected their hands. She nodded and the girls took their place at the table.

"And Georgie?" she asked. But little George was nowhere to be seen. Mrs. McMaster looked toward the girls. "Where's Georgie? If he's out in the barn bothering the horses again, he'll be a sorry little boy."

When neither of the girls seemed to know his whereabouts, Mrs. McMaster let a sharp "George McMaster!" fly out of her mouth. I was about to offer to go search for him when he charged into the kitchen and stopped abruptly in front of his grandmother. She looked at him through her knitted brow.

"Hands, please." He stretched his palms out and turned them over for her scrutiny. "Very good. Now, please sit." He quickly climbed onto his chair. "In the future, if you're not here on time, you'll go to bed without supper. Now, sit up straight."

Mr. McMaster sat down at the head of the table and carved the meat before any other food was served. After he had taken what he wanted from the plate, he passed it to Trent, who then sent the plate around the table. It was the same with the vegetables. Each time something was passed, a polite "thank you" followed. It was a far cry from the meals at our house, with everyone talking at once and hands helping themselves to the food. Not to mention the occasional burp, causing Mama to scold and the rest of us to laugh. That behaviour would never be tolerated at the McMasters' table.

Mr. McMaster watched me in silence. As if working under the wary eye of his mother wasn't bad enough, having Mr. McMaster observing my every move was even more unnerving. I couldn't figure out if he approved of me or not. Some people you can tell just by the looks of them what they're thinking, but not so with Mr. McMaster. I can't say that he looked cross, nor can I say he looked pleasant. If I had to best describe the look on his face, I'd say it was one of indifference, as if he wasn't sure what to make of the girl Brock Cameron had landed on his doorstep that morning.

"So, Lark," he finally said, dipping into the mashed potatoes, "how was your first day here? Are you getting settled in?"

"Yes, sir, I am," I answered nervously, my words coming out as shrill as a train whistle. Martha, Sylvie, and Georgie jumped; even I jumped. Mrs. McMaster's eyes grew wide. Too late to clamp my hand over my mouth. The damage had been done.

"It's hardly reason for shouting at the supper table. Now, quiet down this minute," said Mrs. McMaster. "You'll find in this house that is totally unacceptable. I'm not sure what all your mother allows, but those things are not and will not be tolerated here."

I swallowed hard. Reaching for my fork, I fumbled and it clattered noisily to the floor. Mr. McMaster shifted uncomfortably.

"And for goodness' sake, get yourself a clean fork from the drawer," said Mrs. McMaster as I was about to wipe the fork off with my napkin.

My skin burned like a piece of coal in the firebox. I prayed for a strong wind to come along and blow me away. Everyone watched as I went for another fork. Trent looked amused. His brother barely took notice and went right back to eating. Martha hid her face in her hands. Sylvie, eyes big as saucers, seemed to be asking what would happen next. Little George began to giggle.

"Georgie, that's enough. There's to be no laughing at this table," barked his father. "You come here to eat, not behave like a clown."

"But Lark is funny," little George said.

"I don't care what Lark is. She's the hired girl," his father said, sending me a cold look as if I were to blame for Georgie's outburst. "She is not here to make you laugh. She is here to work."

The smile disappeared from little George's face and I felt his embarrassment. He squirmed in his chair. "And sit still," Mr. McMaster barked again. "Haven't you learned any manners yet? You're five years old. You ought to have a little sense."

My heart sank at the sad look that crossed little George's face. We sat silently, looking from one to another. Not a single word was whispered. I believe we were all afraid to open our mouths, except to put in the food, of course.

Later, while I was washing the supper dishes, Mr. McMaster opened the kitchen door. He cleared his throat before speaking.

"I don't want you being a bad influence on little George. We are trying to teach the children manners. I don't want you undermining that. Do you understand?"

My bottom lip quivered slightly. "Yes, Mr. McMaster."

As he left the kitchen, his words echoed on in my mind. I promised myself right then and there, I wouldn't go out of my way to make friends with him no matter what. He was cruel and cold. If he couldn't make some allowances for a girl who had only just started working for him that very day, then I knew there couldn't be but a speck of kindness in him. Anger continued to simmer inside me. But then I had another thought. Mrs. McMaster was the person responsible for hiring me, the person who looked after the goings on in the house, not her son Mr. McMaster. He might not like me, but perhaps I didn't need his good opinion. All I had to do was win Mrs. McMaster over before my three-week trial was up.

"Take that, George Stanley McMaster," I said as I quietly scoured the dishes.

CHAPTER SEVEN

WHEN THE LAST SUPPER DISH WAS WASHED AND PUT AWAY, AND THE dirty dishwater dumped over the golden glow out back, Mrs. McMaster excused me for the day.

"I'm sure you're tired. You may go off to your room," she said, and I pretended to see a dash of kindness in her eyes when she looked at me.

"Thank you, Mrs. McMaster. It has been a long day," I admitted. A few words of encouragement would have been welcomed, but that wasn't to be.

"I'll expect you to be up at the crack of dawn tomorrow morning," she added as I headed out of the kitchen. "You may start the day at six. I do hope you're not a sleepyhead."

I turned back toward her. "Oh no, ma'am. I'm usually up before old Red—he's our rooster back home. He's a little cranky sometimes and you have to watch out for him when you're in the dooryard, but he's the best crower we've ever had, which is really the most important thing for a rooster to be and the reason Mama says she keeps him around."

"Up before the rooster crows? I suppose that awaits to be seen. I'll only call the once, mind you. Now run along," Mrs. McMaster said, waving her hand at me. As I hurried off, she let out an exasperated sigh.

If only there was something I could say that she would approve of. Everything that came out of my mouth made me wish I hadn't spoken at all. She'd likely prefer it if I kept all my words to myself. I knew it would be quite impossible for me. Besides, how would she get to know me if I didn't speak? Miss Jollymore said that one day I'd have all my words used up, and when that day came, the world will be a quieter place. That might almost sound like a hateful thing for someone to say, but she smiled when she said it and I knew she really didn't mind how much I talked. With Mrs. McMaster, I couldn't find anything to talk about that was to her liking. Perhaps she was one of those rare people who don't enjoy talking. Imagine how lonely a world you'd live in without the sound of someone's voice to keep you company.

I climbed the stairs to my room, more tired than I'd have thought possible. I decided not to let Mrs. McMaster's constant grouchiness put me into a bad mood. That just wouldn't do. I stopped to look at the photo of the children's mother. Martha and Georgie had no memories of her at all, and Sylvie seemed like a girl who could use a mother's guiding hand. I was sure Mrs. McMaster was doing her best, but it didn't seem like her son was even trying. Couldn't he see that with their mother gone, the children needed him all the more?

As I continued on to my room, I couldn't help feeling sorry for the children. This spacious house they lived in held so much sadness and grief.

"You have arrived at the little room, my dear," I said in my best British accent. I gave a small curtsy and opened the door. Once inside, I took out the stationery Mrs. Hobbs had given me. I wanted to let Mama know I'd safely arrived, but then realized Brock would tell her that I was settled in. I'd wait to write Mama when I had more to say.

Yawning, I pulled back the curtain and looked out across the landscape below me. When we drove up that morning, I saw another house not far from the McMaster homestead and we'd passed several more along the way. From my bedroom window I couldn't see any farmhouses. My room overlooked the dooryard. I could see the barn, trees, and pastureland. Cattle were out grazing and in the far corner was a brown horse standing beside the stonewall. My heart swelled as I thought of Jim.

Below me, children's voices filled the dusk. Martha and George were playing tag in the dooryard. This was the place I was bound to spend the next three weeks, much longer if everything went according to my plan. Would it eventually feel like home? I pondered that question while watching the children play. When Mrs. McMaster called for them to come inside and get ready for bed, I looked about for Sylvie. She wasn't playing with Martha and little George. I saw her then, standing by a large maple tree, looking up at me. I waved at her and she looked quickly away. Her grandmother called her name and she ran toward the house.

Sighing, I got ready for bed. I slipped beneath the covers, my eyelids growing heavy. As I drifted into sleep, I wondered, would I be here long enough to win Sylvie over?

CHAPTER EIGHT

MY FIRST CHORE THE NEXT MORNING WAS TO HELP GET EVERYONE FED and out the door; the men to the hayfield and the girls to their first day of school. Mrs. McMaster roused little George from his bed once everyone had headed off for the day. He ate a quick breakfast and she sent him outdoors to play. When I looked out the kitchen window, he was sitting on the swing, his head drooped and his feet dangling in the dirt; the sorriest-looking boy out for a swing that I had ever seen.

Midmorning, Mrs. McMaster glanced out one of the kitchen windows and let out a soft groan. "For the love of creation. Here comes Bertha Gray up the drive," she said. I caught sight of a woman heading toward the house. She looked determined, her arms swinging as she marched along. She was short and stocky, not much taller than Mrs. Hobbs. Mrs. McMaster looked around the kitchen, at the unwashed dishes stacked up on the table.

"Hurry, Lark, and put on the kettle. She'll expect tea. I'll go to the front door and steer her into the parlour. You did get the parlour cleaned?" She wiped her hands on her apron and, pulling it over her head, handed it to me. She felt for any loose strands of hair.

"Yes, ma'am," I said, baffled by her behaviour. Mrs. McMaster looked none too happy at the thought of company coming. Mama enjoyed having the neighbours drop in for a visit.

"Good. Then you can serve us there. And put some sweets on a plate." She paused. "The molasses cookies, the ones in the red tin. I'm not going to waste my good white cake on her. There's a tray on the bottom shelf in the pantry," she continued. "And mind you don't take too long, Lark Harnish. I simply can't listen to Bertha Gray all morning. There's work to be done…Of all the things," she said, shaking her head.

Her face was lined with apprehension and I wasn't sure why. I'd spent an hour dusting and sweeping the parlour to her speci-fications. The house looked perfect, better than perfect. No one, not even this Bertha Gray she spoke of, could be *that* fussy. Why, if Mama had such a grand house to look after, she'd be happy to welcome company.

"Stay in the kitchen until I come for you, and by all means, keep little George out. Do you understand? I do not want him barging into the parlour. Bertha Gray is far too inquisitive for her own good. It would please her to no end if she had some juicy story to spread far and wide. In the meantime, you can wash these dishes and then start the biscuits for supper. There's a recipe book in the closet, and mind you keep the fire hopping."

Mrs. McMaster sounded uneasy, but I was certain all would go well. Bertha Gray was one person, and Mrs. McMaster's neighbour at that. Neighbours are the people you turn to when you need a helping hand. Mama used to say if it hadn't been for the help of our neighbours, she couldn't have managed when

Papa passed away. They showed up with food and offers to help out in every way they could think of.

"I'm sure everything will be fine," I said, trying to ease her apprehension. Mrs. McMaster did not strike me as someone who would be intimated by anyone.

"It will be as soon as Bertha Gray is fed and on her way home. Now hurry along," she said. She turned quickly on the heels, saying how she shouldn't have to be pestered this early in the day by Bertha Gray, no less. I smiled. Surely, it was just part of Mrs. McMaster's cantankerous disposition. No one could be that bad.

A knock came at the door and Mrs. McMaster went to answer it, grumbling all the way. I filled the dishpan with water, and when I heard her say, "Bertha, my dear, how nice of you to come," I smiled—how nice, indeed.

As I went about my kitchen chores, I was comforted by the sound of their murmured voices in the parlour. It was far better than the quiet of yesterday morning, when the house seemed deserted. When it came time to serve the refreshments, I placed the tray on a little table between the two women. Mrs. McMaster poured the tea. I handed a cup and saucer to Mrs. McMaster's guest and she took a quick sip, looking up at me with curiosity.

"Would you care for a cookie?" I asked, holding the plate before her.

"Someone said you were getting a hired girl, Nadine," she said, smiling. "Pretty little thing, I must say." I returned her smile and felt my skin flush. "I can appreciate a girl who knows her place," she said, still smiling. "What's your name, dear?"

"Lark, ma'am, Lark Harnish." I couldn't imagine why Mrs. McMaster had been so put off by Bertha Gray coming to visit. She seemed friendly enough. She reached for a cookie. I held out the plate to Mrs. McMaster, but she declined with a wave of her hand.

"My, what an interesting name," said Mrs. Gray, biting into her cookie. "What parts are you from?"

"Crawfordville," I replied.

"That's not so very far from here. Ten miles, maybe? We have friends in Crawfordville, down the Walsh Road," she said. "I'm sure you'll be an asset to Nadine."

I took note of the gratified look on Mrs. McMaster's face. Surely, it was a good sign. Mrs. McMaster had been worried for nothing. The visit was going fine. When Mrs. McMaster said I was excused, Bertha Gray stopped me before I could leave.

"Don't run off," she said. "Sit for a moment. I'm sure Nadine has been putting you through the paces this morning. It won't hurt to take a break." She patted a spot on the settee beside her. I looked toward Mrs. McMaster and she gave a small nod. I set the plate of cookies on the tea table and took a seat beside Bertha Gray. She smiled. Mrs. McMaster, on the other hand, seemed less than pleased.

"Now whereabouts in Crawfordville do you live?"

"Back the Stanley Road," I said, but Bertha Gray kept talking to Mrs. McMaster, ignoring my answer to her question.

"Did I tell you about that girl Henny Richardson hired last year, Nadine? She used to make me nervous, always yakking and never doing her work. Your Lark here is quiet. I like that."

Mrs. McMaster raised a curious eyebrow. "I'm afraid we never crossed paths. I haven't been to Henny's in a very long time." Mrs. McMaster sipped her tea in a ladylike fashion.

"I must say, I was happy when Henny sent that girl on her way," Bertha continued.

I sat beside Mrs. McMaster's visitor, not knowing what to do. A silent glare from Mrs. McMaster ordered me to stop nervously swinging my legs, which I hadn't even realized I was doing. I immediately froze. Bertha Gray was too busy talking to have taken notice.

"I warned Henny that first day, but she wouldn't listen. And then the girl bit into a block of cheese...a block of cheese, mind you...when everyone was out of the house, left her teeth marks into it, of all the things. Then went about her day unabashed, as if she thought her deed would go unnoticed."

"My land, why didn't she simply use a knife?" said Mrs. McMaster.

"That's exactly what I said," continued Bertha Gray.

"She had only to ask for a taste of cheese. I'm sure Henny wouldn't have minded. Perhaps it was one of the children," said Mrs. McMaster. "It sounds like something a child would do."

"There was no denying whose teeth marks they were. She was as bucktoothed as a Billy goat. They made the perfect imprint. Philip wanted to match them up, but she refused to cooperate."

She reached toward the tea table and took another cookie from the plate, and I thought I'd burst out laughing right then and there. Mrs. McMaster would never forgive me if I did. I shifted in my seat, lest I'd start laughing and embarrass Mrs. McMaster. It was the funniest story I'd heard in a long while.

"Now get this!" said Bertha, pointing her finger. She looked as though she were about to release the secret of the century. Mrs. McMaster continued to look unimpressed. "I caught her outside the door one afternoon when Henny and I were having tea. Imagine that, if you will. Of course, this was before the cheese incident. She had her ear right up to the door. Right up to the door, mind. Up to the door. Did she not understand privacy?"

As she leaned forward, her arms flung outward. Morsels of cookies sprayed from her mouth. Mrs. McMaster eyed the crumbs as they sailed across the room, landing near her feet. Bertha Gray continued with her story, unperturbed by the mess she'd just made. My stomach made a wild lurch as I swallowed the laughter building in me. I bit my cheek, but that did not discourage the hilariousness of Bertha Gray's story. Even with an aching cheek, the story was one of the funniest I'd heard in ages. Worst of all, Bertha Gray had no idea of how incredibly comical it was.

"I'd like to know what she thought she'd hear; some gossip she could use to discredit poor Henny in the community, no doubt." She rolled her eyes toward Mrs. McMaster as a small noise finally escaped me. I jumped to my feet, quickly asking Mrs. McMaster if there was anything else I could get her. My only reprieve would come if I were able to escape the parlour. If I didn't get out soon, I'd be rolling on the floor, laughing. Mrs. McMaster would have my head for sure.

Trying not to bolt from the room, as I was sure Mrs. McMaster would not approve of such rudeness, I was relieved when she said I should gather up the teacups and leave.

"There is plenty in the kitchen to keep you busy," she said. The women passed me their empty teacups and I placed them on the tray. Bertha Gray kept rambling on about Henny's hired girl.

"Some might say it was Henny's own fault," she said as I offered her the last cookie on the plate before leaving. I needed to stop thinking about that poor girl's teeth marks in the cheese. Bertha declined the cookie, indicating she was full, and kept on talking.

I would never have guessed that the atmosphere in a room could change so abruptly, but when Bertha Gray suddenly said,

"Some are saying it's a frivolous thing, hiring a girl to do the household chores," the urge I'd felt to laugh just moments before dissolved on the spot. I glanced at Mrs. McMaster, who did not look one bit pleased by this statement. I was astounded by Bertha Gray's brashness as she glanced cheekily at Mrs. McMaster. How quickly the visit had soured. All I could think about was hurrying off to the kitchen.

"Some might say it is no one's business," Mrs. McMaster stated firmly. She looked to be on the threshold of losing her temper. I hoped to make it out of the parlour before that happened.

"I'm just repeating what some people are saying."

Fumbling, I grabbed for one of the teacups, catching it moments before it landed on the floor. Silence followed. Mrs. McMaster turned an off-shade of red. The floorboards out in the hallway squeaked and I caught sight of Georgie sneaking past the open curtains. Drat. If only I had thought to close them. Luckily, Mrs. McMaster was so caught up in her anger that she didn't take notice of little George. She had given strict orders for him to stay out of Bertha Gray's path. I now knew why. Bertha's friendly smile had been an act.

Anxious to round up Georgie, I picked up the tray just as Mrs. McMaster began speaking. "I can assure you, Bertha, were it not for the post office I could manage this house just fine on my own. But there is only so much one person can achieve in the run of a day, no matter who they are. The children are a handful on their own."

"Children *are* busy little creatures. What is it they say—at least they're healthy? But there is a price we pay when we overextend ourselves. And to what end, Nadine?" The look of displeasure remained splayed across Mrs. McMaster's face as I headed toward the doorway with the tray.

"Children are not creatures," Mrs. McMaster said huffily. Bertha Gray seemed determined to dominate the conversation, and she kept on talking.

"Surely, someone else would have taken the post office on after Prim died, someone with fewer responsibilities. You don't have to be the saviour of the whole community. Unless, of course, George Stanley's business...oh...never mind." She stopped speaking. By that time, I had made it out into the hallway.

"Everything is not done for some monetary gain, Bertha, my dear," I heard Mrs. McMaster say in a crisp voice. To my horror, Georgie came barrelling out of the room where all the letters and parcels were. I hurried toward him with the tray in my hands, the cups and saucers jiggling. I dare not think about what would happen if he got caught in the post office. I whispered his name and he spun around in my direction.

"There have always been two post offices in Upper Springdale," Mrs. McMaster continued as I caught hold of Georgie's collar. I turned him toward the kitchen, balancing the tray with my one hand, while he pleaded for me not to tell his grandmother. I warned him to stay quiet, that I'd keep his secret so long as he promised to never go in the post office again.

"Surely you wouldn't want to trudge all way to the lower part of the settlement to collect your mail, Bertha. Prim's death left a void in this community. When I was asked to take it on, I answered the call—at least until a more permanent solution is found." My hand quivered from the weight of the tray and I hastened my steps. From inside the parlour, Mrs. McMaster's voice grew louder. "Rest assured there's no reason for you to worry about George Stanley. Business is booming, as they say."

I finally made it to the kitchen and was about to set the tray on the table when everything went crashing to the floor. Little George scurried off like a scared cat, leaving me with the broken china scattered at my feet. Within seconds, Mrs. McMaster barged into the kitchen.

"Lark Harnish! What the devil have you done here?" Her voice vibrated thoughout the entire house.

Bertha stood behind her, shaking her head. "What did I tell you, Nadine? What did I tell you? Why, the poor child is no bigger than a minute. What can one expect?" she said, clucking her tongue. It was bad enough that I'd broken the china, worse to have Bertha Gray be witness to my mishap.

"I'm so sorry, Mrs. McMaster. The tray slipped. I couldn't stop it," I stammered.

"Don't just stand there. Start cleaning this mess up, and mind you don't cut yourself," said Mrs. McMaster sternly. I turned over the tray and began picking up the largest pieces of broken china. Turning then to Bertha Gray, Mrs. McMaster said, "I must ask you to leave, Bertha, while I help clean up this mess."

"Well...if you say," harrumphed Bertha. Looking perturbed, she clomped down the hallway. When the front door slammed shut, Mrs. McMaster let out a sigh and went for the broom.

"Stand back," she said, sweeping the small bits of porcelain into a pile while I fell all over myself apologizing.

"You can take the money for the china out of my pay," I offered, not knowing what else to say. The day had been going so well up until now.

"I should think so," said Mrs. McMaster clutching the dustpan.

"I'll work free for a whole week...or two if you'd like. Please, Mrs. McMaster, I—"

"Enough," she said. "Finish mixing the biscuits and stop blabbering. All I can say is, you can thank your lucky stars it wasn't my good china you broke."

I went back to mixing the biscuits, uncertain as to what my fate might be.

"If there's one good thing that came from this, it was ridding the house of Bertha Gray," she muttered. That was something I couldn't disagree with. Something clattered out in the hallway. Setting the broom aside, Mrs. McMaster went to investigate. Moments later, I heard her scolding poor Georgie. She called for him to come back. Little feet scurried past the kitchen with Mrs. McMaster in pursuit. I worried what would happen if she caught up to him.

"I was *not* making up stories," I heard him cry somewhere in the distance. I blamed Bertha Gray for putting Mrs. McMaster in such a crabby mood. In fact, this whole thing was Bertha Gray's fault. I felt sorry for little George, who was bearing the brunt of his grandmother's scorn as I put the biscuits in the oven.

That night, tired and weary, I put on my nightdress and started to write Mama a letter. There were so many emotions inside me, I had to get them all out. I told her all that had happened that day, from Bertha Gray's ridiculous story to catching Georgie coming out of the post office and the broken china. I told her it was probably a good sign that I was still here and that Mrs. McMaster had not threatened to send me home. Yawning, I placed the letter on my nightstand. I'd finish it tomorrow evening. I was so tired I could hardly think straight let alone remember all the things I had to tell Mama. There would be plenty of time to finish the letter. The mail wouldn't go until Friday, when Brock Cameron came back with his buggy. As I crawled beneath the covers, a squeak outside my room caught my attention. The door was open a bit. Someone was standing outside. A quick flash of green through the crack told me it was Sylvie.

CHAPTER NINE

WHEN FRIDAY CAME, MR. MCMASTER SURPRISED ME AT BREAKFAST.
"I need you in the field to rake in hay this afternoon, Lark Harnish," he said. Unused to him sending even a thimbleful of words my way, I wasn't altogether sure he'd been talking to me until he spoke my name.

"Rake in hay?" Mrs. McMaster repeated as if it were the most ludicrous thing she'd ever heard. "What can she do, George Stanley? It's too hard a work for someone her size. Besides, she's a girl."

"She's here to help, and help she will," Mr. McMaster stated as he gulped the last of his tea.

While Mrs. McMaster sounded none too happy about this, I hoped she wouldn't change his mind. Raking hay sounded like fun.

"She's here to help in the house," corrected Mrs. McMaster. "She's not a field hand. Go ask that boy of Everett Campton's. He's a big strapping lad."

"And haying for Joshua Miller these days—can you handle a hay rake?" he asked, scowling.

"Yes, Mr. McMaster." While I'd never raked hay in the past, I'd scraped together plenty of leaves. I couldn't think there would be much difference. It might be fun to be outdoors for the afternoon. Trent and Firth would most surely be there and Trent could tell his share of stories, many of them funny. I was certain it would prove to be more enjoyable than doing house chores with Mrs. McMaster watching my every move, even if Mr. McMaster came along. The outdoors is plenty big. I'd have no problem steering clear of him. Besides, there was nothing in the hayfield that I could break.

"The hay is dry, now. I want to get it in the barn before the weekend. We'll need all hands, Mother," said Mr. McMaster.

With pursed lips, Mrs. McMaster gave a small nod. "She'll need something appropriate to wear. I'm sure there are still clothes upstairs from when you were a boy," she said reluctantly. Mr. McMaster pushed his chair away from the table and headed toward the porch. Firth and Trent followed.

"You might have discussed this with me first," she said as Mr. McMaster headed toward the porch. If he heard her, he did not let on.

Mr. McMaster took us out to the hayfield shortly after dinner. I was wearing the shirt and trousers that Mrs. McMaster presented me with that morning.

"I won't have George Stanley turning you into a field hand," she'd said as I hurried to try them on. "This is a one-time thing."

I quickly put on the clothes and rolled up the shirt sleeves and the pant legs. The pants, I held in place with a piece of rope. I'm sure I was a funny-looking sight, but I didn't care. When I came back downstairs, Mrs. McMaster told me to hurry or the men would leave without me.

"Come along," said Firth, helping me up on the wagon as the horses began to move.

Our feet dangled over the edge of the hay wagon while Mr. McMaster drove the team down the main road to the field. We passed several farmhouses along the way. Smiling, I wondered if one of them belonged to Bertha Gray.

"What's tickling you?" asked Trent. I shook my head. That story was between me, Mrs. McMaster, and now Mama. Drat! I remembered the letter I'd written to Mama. I'd finished it last evening. I'd been so excited at the thought of helping with the hay I'd forgotten to give it to Mrs. McMaster this morning. Now it wouldn't go until Tuesday, when Brock returned. Mama wouldn't get my letter until late next week. I took a big breath. A late letter was better than no letter. Mama would understand. I was glad now that I hadn't sealed it. I could tell her about my adventure making hay.

Finally, the wagon turned off the main road onto the field of cut hay. Some of the hay had already been gathered off the field, the rest raked into windrows waiting to be stooked into piles and pitched onto the wagon. The sun was bright and the scent of fresh-made hay surrounded us.

I thought then of those hot summer days when Papa would pull up to the barn with a big load of hay on back of the wagon, and how Midge and I would run out to meet him. The neighbours all helped each other bring in the hay. Even Cooper helped when he was old enough. It was fun watching them use the hayfork and pitcher to put the hay in the mow. None of it would have been possible without Jim's help. Once it was in the barn, we'd climb the ladder into the haymow and crawl deep into the hay. We'd pretend to be kittens hiding from our mother. Midge would meow and pretend to lick her paws and only when Mama called for us to come for supper would we dig our way out. But now that we no longer had animals to feed, our haymow was empty. As I thought of all these things, I realized how much I missed all that now that Papa was gone.

Mr. McMaster's soft command brought the horses to a stop. I jumped from the wagon, eager to get started. When Mr. McMaster stepped down onto the ground, he gave each horse a gentle pat on the neck and quietly praised them. Papa used to say that you can tell a person's disposition by the way they handle a horse. Papa was right about most things, but then he never crossed paths with George Stanley McMaster.

Trent handed me a rake and gave me a quick lesson on what to do. Once the hay was in piles, Mr. McMaster and Firth pitched it onto the wagon with their forks. I was having a grand time until that mean old Mr. McMaster decided to put a stop to my fun.

"Slow down," he barked. "You'll tire yourself out and then you'll be no good to anyone."

My head dropped and I said a quick "Yes sir," but he wasn't through. "Better to work at a steady pace and finish the day than end up dragging yourself home before the day is out. There's no need to show off." He thrust his pitchfork in the hay and moved the wagon ahead. We followed along with our hay rakes.

"Sorry about that," said Trent, which did little to soothe my hurt feelings. Besides, it wasn't up to Trent to apologize for Mr. McMaster's nastiness.

"Why is he always so mean?" I asked, dragging my feet across the stubbled field.

"He's a man with a lot on his mind. But that's not your fault," said Trent.

"Maybe you should tell that to Mr. McMaster," I said. How could someone who was so gentle with horses have such a foul disposition? He wasn't even nice to his own children. All he seemed to do was scold them.

"Cheer up, Miss Lark. Don't let what he said bother you. His bark is much worse than his bite, I promise you." When I failed to perk up, he slapped me lightly on the shoulder and flashed one of his silly smiles. He had such a comical look on this face, I couldn't help smiling. "This is nothing that a good night's sleep won't fix. Things will look better in the morning. They always do."

Late that afternoon, we made it back to the farm with a wagon piled high with hay. Firth gave each horse a bucket of water as they prepared to put the hay in the mow. I ran into the house and washed the dirt from my hands and face. Mrs. McMaster had baked bread that afternoon and the aroma was still drifting around the kitchen. I thought of Mama.

"I'll be back in a minute, Mrs. McMaster," I said, hurrying upstairs. Sylvie was standing in the doorway to her room. She glared at me and huffed.

"You look like a boy in those stupid clothes," she stated before closing her bedroom door.

I quickly pulled my dress down over my head. I hoped Sylvie would soon start being friendly. I hurried to the kitchen. As tired as I felt, I couldn't let on to Mrs. McMaster or she might forbid me to help out in the field again. I went for the plates and began setting the table, aware of Mrs. McMaster watching. She made no mention of the afternoon.

"We'll feed the children first," she said. "And hold supper for the men."

It was with a certain amount of satisfaction that I got ready for bed that night, tired and bedraggled. I thought about the letter for Mama. It wasn't on my nightstand. I searched about and found it on the floor next to my bed. I must have knocked it off the stand when I got dressed in the trousers earlier. I opened the letter back up and added a "PS" at the end: *Today I helped the hired men get in the hay. I even got to dress like one of them. It was fun to spend the afternoon outside in the sunshine. I bet I'll sleep well tonight!*

This time I sealed the letter and set it on the dresser, where I'd be sure to see it tomorrow morning. I was certain Mrs. McMaster wouldn't mind putting it in the post office to be sent out Tuesday. I didn't want to miss the mail again. Snuggling beneath the covers, I thought about how pleased Mama would be when the letter arrived.

CHAPTER TEN

"EVENING RED AND MORNING GREY WILL HELP THE TRAVELLER ON HIS way. But evening grey and morning red will bring down showers upon his head."

On my way to fetch water from the well on Monday morning, I heard Trent rattle out this little saying. Indeed, the morning sky was red as cherry pie.

"I'll give you a hand," he said, coming to my aid. He hooked the bucket onto the end of the well pole.

"Do you think it'll soon rain?" I asked, lifting the well cover.

"The sky never lies," he said, lowering the bucket down into the water. "Tomorrow might end up being a day spent under cover. I can feel it in the air. Can you manage from here?" he asked, handing over the bucket of water. "Firth will think I'm shirking my chores if I don't help hitch up the team."

"I'll be fine," I assured him. "Besides, it'll take a lot of water for all the clothes waiting to be washed."

"You know what they say, Miss Lark, all work and no play makes Jack a dull boy."

"I should be just fine then, because my name isn't Jack." I laughed, carrying the water into the house.

By the time all the whites were boiling on top of the stove, Mrs. McMaster marched into the kitchen and looked down into the tub of laundry. I was sure she'd be pleased with what I'd accomplished. But she curled up her nose and a strange sound escaped her. "What is wrong this time?" I wanted to cry.

"For goodness' sake, at this rate the morning will be half gone before the wash ever makes it to the line. Oh, this will never do." Reaching for the wooden paddles behind the stove, she began taking the clothes out of the hot water. "I always get my wash out before Bertha Gray. Always. Without fail." She placed a steaming-hot shirt into an empty washtub and reached for another. "Now hurry along and get some rinse water from the well." Her words suggested urgency, so I ran outside, determined not to have that old Bertha Gray get her laundry out first. I grabbed the well pole and began lowering the bucket into the well.

"Oh, sugar!" I cried as the bucket slipped off the end of the pole. It bobbed about the water, threatening to fill up and sink if I didn't soon retrieve it.

"Is something the matter?" Mrs. McMaster called.

"Everything is fine," I sang out. Mrs. McMaster might fire me on the spot if I lost her good bucket at the bottom of the well. Some broken teacups would be nothing compared to this. I had to do something quick.

"That nothing of yours seems to be taking you a mighty long time," she called out from the doorway.

"I'll be right along," I answered, frantically trying one more time to hook the handle. But as hard as I tried, I couldn't get a proper hold on it. It didn't help knowing that Mrs. McMaster was in the kitchen, likely stomping her feet and making all sorts of speeches about how long it was taking the hired girl to get a bucket of water from the well.

My persistence paid off and I finally had the bucket hooked when Mrs. McMaster's voice sliced through me. "Now what have you done, Lark Harnish?" I jumped and it jarred loose again. I watched it bobbing about the water.

"I'm afraid I lost the bucket in the well," I said miserably.

"Oh, fiddlesticks!" she said, marching across the grass toward me. "This wouldn't happen if we had a hand pump, I told George Stanley just the other day. Just because no one in Upper Springdale has one, doesn't mean we shouldn't—progress, I told him. Someone needs to be the first."

She grabbed the pole from me and in one swift movement was lifting the bucket, filled with water, out of the well. "I always have my wash out before Bertha," she grumbled, carrying the pail of water into the house. "Today will be no different!"

We took turns scrubbing the clothes. The fabric squeaked across the scrub board. My arms grew tired, but I pushed onward. If someone Mrs. McMaster's age could do it without complaining, then surely I could, too.

True to her word, Mrs. McMaster had the wash ready to be hung shortly before eight thirty. "I trust you've set out laundry before," she said when the clothes were sitting in the basket.

"Thousands of times, I'm sure!" I said eagerly, pleased that we were right on time.

"I hardly believe that to be the truth, Lark Harnish." She shook her head and made a clicking sound with her tongue. "A bit of an overstatement, wouldn't you say?"

While the day appeared perfect on the outside with scarcely a cloud in the sky, things weren't going well at all. I couldn't afford any more blunders. At this rate I'd never make a hired girl. The look on Mama's face when I was sent back home would put her into despair. The grocery bill would never get paid off. We'd forever be in debt.

I picked up the laundry basket and walked toward the clothesline. I let out a sigh. I could hardly tell Mrs. McMaster that, in my attempt to be enthusiastic about something as mundane as hanging out clothing, I most surely had exaggerated. I wasn't deliberately setting out to be boastful.

"No need to dilly-dally," said Mrs. McMaster from the doorway. "The day is growing old and there is baking to be done."

I reached for one of the clothes pegs and pushed it in place. I wasn't ready to give up. When the last of the clothes were pinned onto the line, I searched around the grass for the clothesline pole. The line fit perfectly into the notch at the top. I pushed the line up into place, where the sun and wind could do the rest. The clothes looked so beautiful hanging on the line, like a string of colourful flags flapping gently in the breeze. Surely Mrs. McMaster would be satisfied with me this time. I gathered up the basket and headed toward the house feeling as pleased as any one person could when it came to hanging out laundry. But no sooner had I made it back into the kitchen than Mrs. McMaster began to wail.

"Look what you've done now, Lark Harnish," she stammered, her both hands resting on the window sash. I raced to her side, to see what had her so upset. The pole that had been holding the line of clothes had fallen to the ground, and my beautiful line of clothes was dangling in the dirt.

"I'm so sorry, Mrs. McMaster. I don't know how this could have happened. I was so careful." I could feel the weight of her judgment once again.

"Sorry indeed…'Don't know how it happened'…'I was so careful.'" She moved away from the window wearing a most distasteful look.

"What will we do?" I asked. The clothes would most surely be soiled.

"Do? Why, you'll have to gather them in and start from scratch."

"Start from scratch!" I howled.

"You must learn not to yell when things don't go your way, Lark Harnish," she said with a sour look on her face. "It's most unbecoming."

"But all that time and work," I moaned.

"There's no sense crying over spilled milk. And next time it's best to admit when you don't know how to do something. I would have shown you the proper way. But you knew better."

I tried to explain that I really did know how to hang out clothes, that this had been an unfortunate accident, but she wasn't interested.

"Enough of your excuses," she said as we headed for the sagging clothesline. "It's always best to do something right the first time, Lark Harnish. If you learn that much, you'll be doing something. A thousand times, indeed!" she griped.

I took a deep breath and began removing the clothes. "I'll try harder next time, Mrs. McMaster," I promised.

"That's all I can pray for at this point," she said as we carried the basket of soiled clothes back into the kitchen. "And if Bertha

Gray has anything to say about this when I see her down at Ramey's store, I'll just tell her to blame the hired girl."

I headed for the well with the water bucket, more determined than ever to do things the proper way. That's all I could do for now.

CHAPTER ELEVEN

EARLY THAT AFTERNOON, THE DISTANT SKY FILLED WITH MASSIVE STORM clouds that looked to be heading our way. As the afternoon wore on, the sun disappeared. A strong gale whipped across the pasture, blowing the clothes on the line high into the air. We hurried out to gather them in before the rain came down. Struggling to catch hold of the line, it flipped and flapped high in the air. Finally, I grabbed hold of it, pulling it down where it could be reached. I steadied it while Mrs. McMaster removed each item.

"I was hoping the rain would hold off until tomorrow," she said, dropping the wooden pegs into her apron pocket. I placed the folded clothes into the basket and pulled it along. We worked our way down the line. I was determined to do something to her liking. She had the power to send me home if my work wasn't suitable. But as much as I wanted to please her, it seemed she was beyond pleasing.

"Trent said we were in for a storm," I said when the last shirt went into the basket. "The sky was so red this morning. He had a little saying that went with it."

"Trent can rattle off a whole string of those sayings. I sometimes wonder where he keeps them all. He's not the brightest star in the sky," she said. I laughed but stopped abruptly when Mrs. McMaster gave me a stern look. I thought she had been joking. "You must learn to stop that nervous laughter of yours, Lark. It's most unladylike. Do you want people to think your mother raised you without any manners?"

"Why no, Mrs. McMaster." I was never told that laughing was impolite. "Mrs. Hobbs says a good laugh lifts the heart and people who laugh often, live longer."

"I hardly think a little laughter can be attributed to longevity. My mother lived to be ninety-three. She was far too busy working to be playing the fool, and for the life of me I can't remember ever hearing her laugh. Now come along. The men are in the woods today and will be soaked if they don't soon hurry home." Mrs. McMaster headed toward the house with the wash basket in her arms. "I expect there will soon come a downpour."

I no sooner had the door closed than large water drops splashed against the window.

The smell of turnip kraut filled the kitchen. Georgie sat by the window watching the rain wet the windowpane. I always enjoyed the sound of the rain on our roof at home. Sometimes it would drip down into the loft where Midge and I slept. Mama would bring up one of her pots to catch the drips. The raindrops made music as they hit that empty pan. Ping...ping...plop! Lying in bed, Midge and I would put words to the notes before drifting off to sleep.

Outside, the rainwater poured into a large wooden barrel that sat beneath the eaves. "Can I play in the water barrel tomorrow?" asked Georgie, squeaking his hands across the cool glass.

"Certainly not!" snapped Mrs. McMaster. "Rain water has many uses, the least of which is to entertain little boys. It'll save the job of getting water from the well come wash day."

Little George laid his cheek against the window and groaned.

"For heaven's sake, sit up straight and stop smearing your hands over the windows," said Mrs. McMaster, looking over at him.

Georgie sighed and shifted in his chair. "When's Papa coming home?" he asked restlessly.

"When Papa gets good and ready. Can't you find something to do? Your sisters are home from school—why don't you go play with them? You make me nervous." I was beginning to see that Mrs. McMaster was most cross when she was in the middle of doing something, which was most of the time. She didn't like interruptions, especially when she was busy. It was proving to be a challenge, knowing when was the best time for me to speak and when to let her do the talking.

Despite what his grandmother said, Georgie remained at his spot by the window. Mrs. McMaster brought out a plate filled with cookies and cake and set it on the kitchen table. Never a meal went by at the McMaster home without sweets on the table, even for breakfast. Some people like to say that sweets make you sweet. If that were true it should make the McMasters the sweetest family in all of Upper Springdale, maybe even the world.

Little George made a sorry-looking sight sitting by the window with a face full of longing. I didn't want him to think everybody in the household was annoyed with him. He wasn't doing anything that deserved a scolding. He was inquisitive was all, with an imagination he was only just beginning to find. Miss Jollymore said imagination is what brings progress to the world. I knew she was right. Without imagination many things would never have been invented. As I brought the stack of plates out of the pantry, I looked over at Georgie and winked. He smiled, then looked out the window toward the barn once again.

"Firth says he's going to learn me how to ride on Charlie's back." Little George squirmed in his chair as he waited for the men to come out of the woods.

"That sounds like fun. Who's Charlie?" I asked, setting the plates around the table.

"Papa's horse out in the pasture. He's too old to work." I had yet to be properly introduced to Charlie, but I'd been watching him from my window most evenings at bedtime. "When I learn how to ride," Georgie continued, "Firth's going to take me on a journey to a faraway land. We're going to have a picnic and—" His eyes were shining.

"Georgie," Mrs. McMaster scolded. She was frowning. "Time and again I've told you not to make up stories. Firth has more than enough to do without wasting his time playing with the likes of you. Now sit there and stop making up fairy tales, or I'll put you to bed without supper." Little George groaned. The disappointment on his face crushed my heart as I placed the forks and knives around the table. The kitchen remained quiet for a time as we waited for the sound of boots in the porch.

"They're back!" George suddenly cried out, making a jump off the chair he was sitting in.

Mrs. McMaster marched over to the window. "So they are," she said, glancing outside. "And looking like drowned cats, I might add. Oh, the mess they'll make on our floors, Lark. You'll be down on your hands and knees at the crack of dawn tomorrow morning. Darn that Trent and his old saying."

"Trent and his saying...Trent and his saying," squealed Georgie. He ran out to the porch, anxious for the men to come in.

"Hush now," scolded Mrs. McMaster once again. I stuck the potatoes.

The gentle sound of the rain reached me when Georgie opened the porch door. Mrs. McMaster quickly closed it and pulled him into the kitchen.

"Can I go into the barn to see the horses?" Hope skipped across his face and his cheeks were swollen out like a chipmunk's as he smiled up at his grandmother.

"I would hardly think the men would want you underfoot. There's work to be done, hames and collars and harnesses to be removed. There's nothing you can do. Besides, you could get trampled by those wretched beasts. Now, go sit down and be quiet."

When Sylvie wandered into the kitchen, Mrs. McMaster wasted no time asking her to take little George out of her way. "He's being a nuisance. At this rate it'll be midnight before we eat. Go get him washed up for supper—all of you."

"Come with me, Georgie, there's some water in the basin out in the hallway." Sylvie took him by the hand, but he braced his feet.

"I don't want to wash my hands," he kept saying as Sylvie pulled and tugged at him. Mrs. McMaster began dishing up the food and I heard Sylvie calling for Martha. I took the biscuits out of the oven. I could hear the men talking and the thumping of their boots as they came into the porch. Little George was still protesting.

"Hush now, Georgie," Sylvie said in the distance. "Do you want Papa to scold you again?"

Mr. McMaster rolled his eyes at me then took his place at the table. I thought maybe he was about to say something but had suddenly come up shy. I smiled, but he sat blank-faced as if he couldn't fathom the idea that my smile might have been meant for him. A strange feeling came over me then as Mr. McMaster sat scowling. No wonder his children seemed sad so much of the time. He couldn't even manage a smile. I regretted my attempt to be friendly, but I refused to let his dark mood affect me.

Reaching for a warm biscuit, he pulled it apart. "There's too much soda in the biscuits. They're yellow inside. Lark, is this your doing?" he barked.

Mrs. McMaster stopped dishing up the turnip kraut. An odd expression crossed Mr. McMaster's face when she said, "I mixed the biscuits, George Stanley. Lark just took them out of the oven."

CHAPTER TWELVE

"THERE'S AN ART TO PRESSING PROPERLY," MRS. MCMASTER SAID AS SHE rubbed the hot iron onto a catalogue page. The paper curled and turned brown. She held it there for a few moments, waiting for the iron to cool down, before placing it against the pressing cloth. Being mail day I had offered to do the ironing, but Mrs. McMasters insisted on doing it herself, even if that meant waiting for evening.

"Too much heat will scorch. Not enough and you may as well rub your hand over it. Perhaps someday you'll learn how."

"Indeed, Mrs. McMaster, I'm always willing to learn new things. Miss Jollymore, the teacher back home, says a person should always be looking around for new experiences. Life just ends up being the same old thing every day if you don't."

"Yes, well, there's much to be said for a certain amount of routine. This Miss Jollymore of yours sounds a bit on the fickle side," she replied curtly. "Hand me that dress, please."

She spread it out on the ironing board. "With that attitude I would suspect in a few months you'll have run out of these new experiences you're talking about. You'll have done most everything there is in the house...Then what? Will you move off to some other place and stay only so long as things are new?"

A few months? Did this mean what I thought it meant? I didn't dare get my hopes up. I had just made it past the first week of my trial period. There were still two weeks to go.

"I'm sure it will take a long time for that to happen," I said eagerly.

"We'll see then, won't we? But don't expect that we'll go out of our way to entertain you, Lark Harnish. You're here for one thing and one thing only—to help me. I hope you remember that when everything is old."

From the corner of the kitchen, Georgie watched me measuring out flour. Eyes wide with curiosity, he didn't make a peep. With Sylvie and Martha at school, there was little for him to do all by himself.

"Don't just stand there, come on over and keep me company," I said, adding a teaspoon of salt to the flour. "I won't bite, you know."

The moment I spoke, he raced out the door as if there were a fire at his heels. But the next morning, as I was preparing to wash dishes, he was standing in the corner of the kitchen, looking like a boy who had something to say only he didn't know where to start.

"I'm glad you decided to come back for a visit. I get lonely working by myself." I didn't look up from my work, afraid I'd spook him again if I did. He put me in mind of Jim right after Papa had bought him, the way he'd flinch whenever someone walked past. It took plenty of patience to convince Jim that we weren't going to hurt him. Once he understood there was no reason to be frightened, he turned out to be the best horse we ever owned.

"I've got a brother about your age. Only he's not nearly as quiet as you. In fact, he's been known to talk a fellow's ear right off."

George let out a giggle. I went about my business, filling the dishpan with hot water.

"It dropped right off into his tea, it did."

"No it didn't!" Georgie's eyes lit up. I had him hooked.

"Indeed, it did. You happen to know the fellow, as a matter of fact." I pushed the dishcloth inside a tumbler and twisted it around.

"Who?" he demanded to know. I looked him over as if deciding whether or not to tell.

"Well, if you must know, it was none other than Brock Cameron. And let me tell you, when you've got ears the size of Brock Cameron's you're likely to know when one goes missing. What happened next was the worse thing yet."

"What? What happened?" asked Georgie, now dancing with excitement.

"Why, it put him off balance. Losing an ear that size will do that to anyone. He fell to the floor, took the teacup and ear with him, which ended up being a good thing. The hot tea spilled down over him and melted his ear right fast to his head again. He was as good as new. No one ever found out, except for the person who was there to witness it all."

"Who was there? Who saw it? Was it you, Lark?"

"You can't very well expect me to break a confidence," I said. "I made a solemn promise never to tell." I could scarcely keep from laughing.

Georgie jumped up and down. "Is that real, Lark?"

I smiled. "Oh, you're a clever lad, aren't you? I'm just teasing. But do you know what? I bet deep down inside you're aching to talk just as much as my brother Frank. Mama says if the good Lord saw fit to provide us with a tongue then we'd be better off to use it. And, believe me, Frank takes full advantage."

"Grandmother says for me to stop chattering all the time."

"I won't tell your grandmother if you don't," I said. I knew exactly how he felt. "Feel free to talk all you want when it's just you and me."

That put the smile back on his face. I know how hard it is not to talk. Why, sometimes I go beside myself when Mrs. McMaster insists I stop jabbering.

CHAPTER THIRTEEN

"HOW DO YOU DO IT, CHARLIE? HOW DO YOU STAND HERE IN THE PASture with the wind blowing over you without a care in the world?" I rubbed Charlie's nose. He flicked his ears and swished his tail.

"Don't you get lonely out here all by yourself without another horse to talk to? I wouldn't think the cows and steers make good company for a horse. Do you even speak the same language? I couldn't stand not having someone to talk to."

I couldn't imagine what it must feel like to be Charlie, standing in the pasture without another horse in sight, but did he even care? I couldn't tell. Maybe he was like Mrs. McMaster; maybe he didn't like the constant jabbering of the cows, that's if cows even jabber, which I think probably they don't.

It was Friday evening. Right after the dishes were done, Mrs. McMaster took out a basket filled with socks that needed darning—a job she said she'd been putting off for the longest time. I had the evening off to do what I wanted. I thought about writing Mama a letter, but when I looked out my bedroom window and saw Charlie standing by the fence, I decided it was high time I made his acquaintance. I'd been with the McMasters more than a week and we hadn't yet been properly introduced. That just wouldn't do. I'd been watching him from my window every evening, standing all by himself in the pasture. He looked so lonely. It made me wonder if horses think, and if they do, what do they think about all day long?

Charlie playfully nudged my shoulder. "I bet you are lonely—aren't you, boy? Well, I'll let you in on a little secret, Charlie. So am I." Charlie pulled back, but then brought his head back to me.

"I know...you think it's different for me. Don't you? And you're right. There are people here for me to talk to and there are only cows out here in the pasture. But some of the people here aren't all that friendly, in case you haven't noticed." Charlie let out a snort and nodded his head in agreement. "Like you and the cows, we don't speak the same language. I'm pretty sure Mrs. McMaster would like it if she never heard me speak again. Every time I open my mouth, the wrong words come out. I know everyone here misses young Mrs. McMaster. But they're stuck in the past, wishing she were still here." I playfully pulled Charlie's ears as I spoke, something Jim liked.

"All they do is make each other miserable, Charlie. Martha is friendly enough, but Sylvie is nasty most of the time. I'm sure it's because she misses her mother. She just wants some attention, someone to be her friend. Her father hardly notices her, any of them. Don't even get me started about how he treats little George."

As I rubbed Charlie's neck, I thought about how much I missed Jim, and how hard it was for Mama to sell him after Papa died. Papa and Jim spent a lot of time together. It was hard to think about Papa without thinking of Jim.

The barn door opened and Firth and Trent appeared in the doorway. Trent called out to me and waved. They'd be leaving bright and early tomorrow morning. They went home on the weekends, which had made things even more lonesome for me on Saturday and Sunday. At least Trent brought his cheerfulness into the house when he came in for supper, not that the McMasters seemed all that pleased when he did. That never stopped him from making conversation, not even those times when he practically had to drag the words out of Mr. McMaster.

"We're going to play a few hands of forty-fives before turning in for the night," Trent said. "You're welcome to join us for a game."

"I'm afraid I don't play cards," I said.

"If you ever want to learn," offered Trent. They both gave a wave before continuing on to the tenement house. Trent and Firth played cards most evenings. I'd overheard Trent invite Mr. McMaster to join them a few times. Instead, Mr. McMaster would sit by the parlour window, smoking his pipe in silence. He'd growl at the children and tell them to quiet down if they so much as let a giggle slip out. Most evenings, Mrs. McMaster sent them outdoors to play and out of their father's way. If only he'd spend time with them, maybe play games in the dooryard the way Papa used to with us.

I waved to Trent and Firth, then turned back toward Charlie. I only wished I had a treat. Jim always knew I'd have something for him. Sometimes I'd hide his treat behind my back and he'd sniff at me, trying to find it. But I didn't have a carrot for Charlie. Some sweet clover was growing on my side of the fence. I pulled a handful and held it out in my open palm. Charlie's lips flapped several times before he picked it up. I patted his neck and starting talking again.

"Papa had a fine horse we called Jim. He was so kind and gentle. Papa would harness him up and take us all into town and in the winter, he'd hitch him to the sleigh. Jim wouldn't hurt a flea. You have his temperament. Do you know that, Charlie?" Charlie softly snorted and nodded his head. I laughed.

"Can I tell you another secret, Charlie? I'm here on a three-week trial and if I don't stop making mistakes Mrs. McMaster won't keep me on when that time is up. Mama needs the money, Charlie. She needs it so badly and I really want to help...I have to help. But sometimes I miss my family so much so that I start thinking maybe I should just go home. The chances of Mrs. McMaster keeping me on aren't all that great, not with all the mishaps that have taken place since I arrived." I swallowed hard, thinking how true this was. Maybe I *should* go home. I pulled in a deep breath until I found my determination. "But I can't go home, Charlie. I just can't, not with everyone depending on me. I've got to make the best of things. I've got to." I nodded, my resolve returning.

Some of the cows were lying down chewing their cud; others were still out grazing. A warm breeze blew across the pasture. Charlie stood listening while I rattled on. I hugged fast to him. I told him what all had happened to me since I'd arrived. I talked about the things I'd been thinking but couldn't say because Mrs. McMaster didn't like to hear me jabber. And I told him all the things I couldn't write in a letter to Mama because I didn't want her to worry. I told him how I closed my eyes in bed at night and pictured everyone back home.

I talked until I didn't have another word left in me, and that's when I heard someone calling my name. I looked around and Martha and Georgie were running toward me.

"What are you doing, Lark?" asked Georgie as he and Martha came to a halt in front of me.

"Why, Charlie and I are having a little chat."

"Horses can't talk," laughed Georgie.

"You'd be surprised what all horses can do," I told him, quickly smiling. Martha and Georgie pulled some clover for Charlie, who took it from their outstretched hands.

"Thank you, Charlie," I said. Rubbing his nose one last time, I looked down at Martha and Georgie. "Now come on, let's go play tag!"

CHAPTER FOURTEEN

"**G**EORGIE PORGIE PUDDING AND PIE, KISSED THE GIRLS AND MADE THEM cry. And when the boys came out to play, Georgie Porgie ran away." Georgie looked up at me and smiled. I don't think he was used to hearing rhymes with his name in them. In fact, I'm sure he wasn't used to hearing rhymes at all. I believe he thought I made it up all on my own. I should have told him that I wasn't nearly that clever.

My second Saturday there, right after supper, Martha and Sylvie stood before their father with their hands outstretched. Mr. McMaster dropped a big round penny into their open palms and away then ran to Mrs. Butler's small store. They came back later, each chewing on a liquorice whip. When Georgie asked for some, Sylvie broke off a small piece and gave it to him.

"That's all you get," she said, running away, taking her candy with her.

"I wish I had a penny," said Georgie once his sweet treat was gone. I held him on my lap and rocked him, hoping to soothe his hurt feelings.

"What would you buy?" I was curious to know.

"Oh, I don't think anything. I'd just like to hold it." The longing in his eyes couldn't be denied.

"Ask your father. He'll give you one."

"Do you think?" He squirmed on my lap.

"Well, I don't see why he wouldn't. It's just a penny. Why, a penny hardly counts...Go on, now," I said, ushering him along.

Georgie slipped down off my lap and headed for the parlour. His father was sitting by the window smoking his pipe. I followed, hoping Mr. McMaster wouldn't send him away disappointed. He only wanted a penny. What harm could there be? George stood before his father and stretched out his hand. This was Mr. McMaster's chance to do something nice for his son.

"Yes?" Mr. McMaster barked, looking down at Georgie's open palm.

"I'd like a penny, too, Papa," he managed to say.

Mr. McMaster didn't stir. The truth is, I'm not at all sure he knew what to do. He sat there like a toad on a mossy rock, as if waiting for a fly to come along so that he could wrap his tongue out around it and yank it into his mouth. I hoped little George wasn't that fly.

"What would you do with a penny? You're too small to go to the store on your own."

Georgie refused to move. "It's just down the Miller Road. Sylvie and Martha get to go," he said.

"Well, that's different," huffed Mr. McMaster.

"Because you like them better?"

"Don't talk so silly. You're five years old. You can't go to the store by yourself, so get that idea out of your head." Mr. McMaster folded his arms in front of him, stubborn as any one man could be. Little George looked as though he might cry. I had to say something. It was my fault for sending him to ask for a penny in the first place.

"I'll take him," I chimed. "It's no trouble at all." George jumped up and down, clapping his hands. I looked at Mr. McMaster, hoping I hadn't made things worse. He sat there red-faced for a spell. Reluctantly, he reached into his pocket and produced a penny for little George. You would have thought he had just given him a hundred dollars the way he went on about money being hard to come by these days and how it wasn't something to be squandered away. I wanted to tell him he was a stingy old goat.

Georgie snatched the penny up as if afraid his father would have a change of heart.

"What do you say for it?" his father demanded.

"Thank you, Papa," replied little George, stopping suddenly. Mr. McMaster nodded. And if the smile little George gave his father wasn't enough to cause Mr. McMaster's old heart to soften, I figured he wasn't deserving of little George's love.

We walked to Mrs. Butler's little store, the sun hanging low in the sky. Georgie carried the penny in his hand, admiring it every once in a while. The sign pointing to the Miller Road could be seen in the distance. When we passed the Grays' farmhouse, I imagined that old busybody, Bertha Gray, was watching us from one of the large bay windows, maybe even wondering what we were up to.

As we turned down the Miller Road, Georgie talked about what all he might buy with his penny. We passed potholes in the road, filled with water from the last rain, and not once did he ask to stop and play in them. That's how determined he was. When we reached Mrs. Butler's, he strutted across the verandah and in through the door. But in the end, he wouldn't spend it, despite Mrs. Butler's attempts to entice him with every type of candy she had. He looked at the candy and then at the money in his hand and he said, "I think I'll keep it for a while."

∞

"How far away is the moon?" asked little George later that evening as we sat in the rocker.

"More than a day's drive by horse, I would imagine."

"Horse?" His eyes grew wide.

"Well, naturally a horse. Now, don't go thinking you could walk all that way by foot. The road to the moon is real dark. It would take a horse's eye to see it properly. Why, a person would squint and strain and end up lost over by the big dipper."

"Papa has his Charlie horse standing in the pasture," said Georgie. "I bet Charlie could find his way to the moon."

"I hardly think so. Old Charlie's not as young as he used to be. That's why your Papa bought that team of his to haul out logs. Besides, Charlie walks far too slowly to ever make it to the moon. Before you'd know it, he'd be off some place taking a nap."

The rockers on the chair creaked steadily as I continued to rock Georgie. "I have no mum," he whispered after a few moments of silence. "It's because of me, too."

"Wherever did you get that idea?" I asked, shocked to hear him speak that way.

"Martha said Mama died when I was born." The sad look on his face tugged at my heartstrings, to think that he'd been carrying this heavy weight in his heart.

"It's not your fault, Georgie," I told him. "It's just the way life works out sometimes. It's no one's fault. Take a look at me. I have no father, and I'm out working to make my way. Sending home money to help out. Life gives us challenges, and it's up to us to decide what to do with those challenges."

"I never got to see her and sometimes I forget," he said sadly.

"Then you'll need to find something to remind you of her," I said.

"Like what?" he asked, looking up at me.

"Well, let me think. The leaves on the winter beech always remind me of Papa because he liked them so much. The year he died, my brother picked some for me. I stuck the limbs into a jar and kept them in my room. Whenever I looked at them, I thought of Papa."

"I don't know what Mama liked," said little George. I tried to think of something, but not knowing anything about his mother, I had nothing to suggest.

"Then you need to keep your eyes and ears open and maybe one day you'll think of something. You have all the time in the world to discover things about your mother. I promise."

"Martha said Papa doesn't like me because of Mama dying," he whispered.

"Of course he likes you. What father wouldn't like their son?"

The look on his face suggested that he didn't believe me. How could I make him understand? His father was a man of few words even at the best of times. He often watched little George in silence as if he just didn't know what to say. The real truth be told—and this came straight from Brock Cameron himself—the day Mr. McMaster's wife passed away, the entire household changed.

"George Stanley was never the same after that," Brock had said. "You ask anyone from these parts. They'll tell you."

CHAPTER FIFTEEN

"THERE'LL BE PLENTY OF SNOW FOR THE SHOVELLING THIS YEAR," SAID Trent as Mr. McMaster passed the potatoes to him. "The hornet nests are up high off the ground." Trent looked across at me and winked.

Mrs. McMaster made a clucking sound with her mouth. "Surely you don't go along with that nonsense, Trent Gates," she said, buttering a slice of bread.

"As sure as I'm sitting here," said Trent, reaching for the gravy. "There have been other signs, too."

"The hornet nests were in the ground last year and we scarcely had enough snow to bank the house," said Mr. McMaster.

Mrs. McMaster gave him a stern look. I'm sure she wanted to tell her son to be quiet, that she had no use for Trent and his old sayings, seeing how he wasn't the brightest star in the sky. Sometimes I wondered if she just wasn't annoyed with Trent's sunny disposition. Perhaps she'd like it better if he was as sober as his brother. Firth usually sat at the table in silence.

"Lark, I suppose your mother has made her pickles by now," said Mrs. McMaster, quickly changing the subject. For the past few days we had been trying to use up all the vegetables in the garden before the frost took them. A crock of salt cucumbers, a half-barrel of pickled cabbage heads, and the last of the green beans were snipped and salted down.

"We had most of the pickles made before I came to work for you. Mama says she can make a meal out of bread and butter if she has pickles to go with it."

Mrs. McMaster screwed up her face and said, "These days I'm as slow as cold molasses."

"It's hardly your fault," I said. "You're busier than most people *I* know."

From the corner of my eye, I saw Mr. McMaster nod his head in agreement. For the most part he'd been ignoring me, which didn't upset me in the least. Some days, dealing with Mrs. McMaster was challenging enough.

"That's hardly an excuse," sighed Mrs. McMaster. "I guess I'm getting old is all."

"You're only old if you think you are." I pitched the words in my most cheerful voice.

"Then I must be ancient," she said flatly, taking a bite of chicken.

After the supper dishes were washed, Mrs. McMaster handed me the dishpan and told me to pick cucumbers.

"Nothing too big and seedy, mind you. And make sure to cover the cucumber patch when you're done. There's bound to be a frost with the full moon tonight."

I'd been covering the cucumbers with blankets before dark. Mrs. McMaster was determined to have them made into pickles before the frost hit.

"I detest waste," she said one day as we sat on the verandah snipping beans. "The winters are long. It's a comfort to know there's plenty in the cellar."

Looking out at the evening sky, I swung the dishpan in my hands as I went along. "Evening red and morning grey will send the hired girl on her way," I sang cheerily as I made my way along. The past few days had gone by quite smoothly. Soon my trial time would be over. The fact that I had made it this far seemed a very good sign. On my way to the garden, I stopped just outside the barn. The stable door was open and I could hear Firth talking to the horses. I'd been longing to see them up close. A few moments wouldn't hurt. The cucumbers could wait.

From inside the stable doorway, I watched Firth slicking the horses' manes. He was putting his whole attention into his work and didn't know I was there. The horses seemed equally unaware of Firth as they munched on their short feed. I cleared my throat and Firth looked my way.

"Can I pet them?" I asked.

"Help yourself."

When I walked up to the front of the stall, one of the horses flapped its lips and snorted.

"This one's named Benny and the other one is Lucky. They like their necks rubbed." Firth was puffed out like a proud mother hen.

"Their coats are so slick," I said, running my hand down across Benny's neck. He stopped eating and brought his head up.

"He knew that wasn't me touching him," said Firth. "Benny's the smartest of the two. He'll do anything you want him to. Lucky just follows."

"Papa used to have a horse. We called him Jim. After Papa died, Mama said it didn't make sense for us to keep him. Jim was used to doing a day's work. Standing in the pasture wouldn't be fair to him."

"Horses are a lot of work, but I'd rather lose my right arm than not have a horse to tend. It was in me from the time I was a boy. Father would sit me on top of our old nag and lead me around the dooryard."

Firth pulled the currycomb across Benny's coat. In another stall Charlie lifted his head and flapped his lips. "Can I brush him?" I asked.

"Charlie's quiet as a whisper. Wouldn't hurt a flea. He doesn't get as much attention as he'd like these days."

"He's good at keeping secrets," I said. "Aren't you, boy?" Charlie looked up at me when I touched him.

"Animals have that way about them," said Firth. "Charlie's got a good life here. From what I hear he did the work of two horses in his day. But don't let him fool you. He's got plenty of kick left in him...Don't you, boy?" Charlie moved his head up and down as if in agreement. I laughed.

Firth pulled a carrot from his pocket and broke it into three parts.

"They could all use a treat," he said. I placed one of the pieces on my open palm and waited for Charlie to take it. His lips flapped several times before he picked it up off my hand. The carrot crunched as he chewed it up. I gave Lucky and Benny the other two pieces.

It was rather nice to hear Firth talking so much. He'd scarcely said a handful of words since I'd come to work for the McMasters. Papa used to say that if you find common ground, you can talk to most anyone. I guess he was right.

"Why, Lark Harnish! I was just about to send a search party out for you." I reeled around. Mrs. McMaster was standing in the stable doorway, her face scrunched up into a tight ball. "Imagine my surprise when I saw my good dish pan sitting right outside the barn. Those cucumbers aren't going to pick themselves, now are they?"

"I'm sorry, Mrs. McMaster, but I so miss the horse Papa used to have. I thought I'd come in for just a quick peek. Jim's been gone so long now. He really was a kind and gentle horse. I know you don't like horses, but not everyone feels that way. Right, Firth?" Firth gave a nod. "I couldn't see the harm in a few minutes. I didn't mean to stay so long, but then Firth and I got to talking. He's really quite good at talking, even though you'd never know it, the way he's always so quiet when he comes to the supper table."

"That's quite enough, young lady! I hardly need to hear Firth's whole life's story. I asked for cucumbers. Heaven only knows why I'd expect as much from you." She stood there shaking her head. "Now come along before the moon comes up and freezes them off."

"I really am sorry for becoming distracted. I'll do better next time," I said, kneeling down in the cucumber patch.

"You must try and complete one task at a time. I can't be following you around. Why, I'm sure a dog could be trained far easier than you, Lark Harnish...Make sure to move the leaves around. They're hard to find." I reached in and pulled out two more cucumbers.

When Mrs. McMaster was satisfied that we'd found all the cucumbers that were ready to be picked, she gathered up the dishpan. I watched her head off to the house. Why couldn't I do things right?

"Are you going to stand there all night?" she asked, turning toward me. "There's still work to be done if we plan to make pickles in the morning, Lark Harnish. Now, come along."

CHAPTER SIXTEEN

IT WAS MOST EXCITING TO HEAR BROCK CAMERON'S BUGGY PULL UP TO the house on mail day, wondering if he had a letter for me. The tiny bells on Bella's harness always announced his arrival. Not long after I wrote Mama to tell her about the episode with Bertha Gray, a letter came for me. I recognized Mama's handwriting as soon as Mrs. McMaster gave it to me. I hurried off to my room and put it away. As excited as what I was, I would wait until evening to open it. I wanted to take my time and savour each and every word.

That evening, I sat down on the bed and took the letter from my nightstand. The envelope was thick and I hugged it to me. Closing my eyes, I imagined I was back home, as if everyone had been folded up and put inside the envelope. Once it was opened, they jumped out to greet me.

"You're looking real grand," I imagined Cooper saying. I pictured him with a pair of horseshoes in his hand, his face and

hands smudged with coal. He was still working at Mr. Nichols's blacksmith shop.

"His arms are sure to be as big around as stove pipes the next time you see him," Mama wrote. Mama was good at keeping me up on all the news.

"Midge is doing just fine in school and is taking her studies quite seriously," Mama wrote next. Immediately Midge popped out from inside the envelope and began rattling off her times tables. I laughed at the notion. I remember Miss Jollymore standing directly in front of Midge last year, asking her if she knew the sum of ten and eight, and Midge was so flustered—what with Miss Jollymore no more than a cat's whisker away from her—she could scarcely count it up on her fingers. I was glad to think that Midge was buckling down and learning her lessons.

"Frank," wrote Mama, *"is up to his usual shenanigans and was darn near caught this time by Jake Palmer, himself. He simply gets more devilish as time goes by. I dread the day he goes off to school. Why, poor Miss Jollymore will have her hair torn out."*

What it was Frank had done, Mama didn't say. Because I missed him so fiercely, I choose not to think of some rotten thing he might have been attempting to do to poor Mr. Palmer. Instead, I imagined Frank, sitting on my bed, looking up at me with those big brown eyes of his. I knew he could have set the house on fire. I wouldn't have had the heart to scold him.

Mama continued,

These September days are growing shorter and soon fall will be here. I strung some apples yesterday to dry behind the stove and I thought of how fond you are of dried apples. But of course you likely don't have the time to remember all those little things. Now, listen to me rambling on about such silliness. If there is anything you need sent from home just let me know. I will send your heavy coat and your winter boots when the weather cools down. Brock will bring them when the time is right. Midge said to tell you that Fluffy brought out three kittens last week. She must have had them hidden away before you even left. Their eyes are open and they're running and scampering all over the barn. Two of them are black and one is orange. The orange one has double paws in front. Cooper says it will make a good mouser. I must go for now.

Love, Mama

Setting Mama's letter aside, I unfolded another note that was inside the envelope. I was from Midge. *"Dear Lark, I miss waking up at night and hearing you sawing wood...Ha...Ha..."*

I smiled. Midge was forever telling me that my snoring kept her awake at night. "I don't know how you could hear my snoring over your own," I used to tell her.

There was a crayon drawing inside the envelope from Frank—some flowers growing beside a river. In the middle of the river was a huge fish because Frank loves fishing more than anyone I know. But the envelope still wasn't empty. There was another slip of paper. I unfolded it. I smiled. It was a note from Cooper.

Today me and Mr. Nichols shod that old red ox of Kyle Manson's, and oh what a time we had to get that ox in the sling. He balked something awful. Mr. Nichols said one of these days he is going to take that ox for a trip back over the pasture, but Mr. Nichols makes threats like that all the time. You'd almost think he didn't like oxen or horses but what blacksmith doesn't like animals? Remember that team Papa had, Bright and Lion, the ones he broke himself from steers? You weren't very old when Papa sold them so maybe you can't remember. But Papa used to let me groom them all the time. Well, that ox of Cliff's has the same marking as Lion. And the minute I saw old Cliff come in with his ox I knew I was going to get myself a team someday, Lark. Just you wait.

Now stay out of trouble and write when you can.

Cooper

Stay out of trouble—his words made me laugh. If only he knew. Cooper's not much when it comes to letter writing, so getting a letter from him was extra special. It was good to hear him excited about something. He was so quiet for the longest time after Papa passed away. I wondered when he'd get back to his old self. Now it seemed that working for Mr. Nichols was doing just that.

When I sat down to write back that Thursday evening I scarcely knew where to begin. There was so much to tell, I was sure I could have filled volumes. I hadn't written since I told Mama about the day Bertha Gray came to visit, and so much had happened since then. I still wouldn't mention my three-week trial. There was no point in worrying her. If Mrs. McMaster ended up letting me go, I'd made up my mind to find some other way of helping Mama out. Besides, Mrs. McMaster hadn't seen fit to scold me in several days, and my trial would be up next week. I could only take that as a good sign.

Dear Mama, Cooper, Midge, and Frank,

I like it here and the time is flying. I can't believe I've been here nearly three weeks. It sounds as if you are all keeping busy, too. Tell Cooper that I can scarcely remember Bright and Lion but I think about Jim quite a little bit. Mr. McMaster has three horses, his hauling team and old Charlie. Some days while I'm washing dishes, I can see Charlie from the window in the kitchen. He stands in the pasture for hours without moving an inch, just his tail swishing some flies out of the way. There are also several milking cows and their calves, and a pig that eats everything in sight. Even Mrs. McMaster likes to go out to the pigpen just to watch it eat. She says the best thing about raising a pig is that nothing ever goes to waste. But she says not to make a pet of the pig for she's seen more than one person crying in their pork chop and mashed potatoes come mealtime. Sometimes Mrs. McMaster has the funniest way of putting things, only she doesn't think it's funny at all.

There are two girls here, Martha and Sylvie, and a boy, Georgie. (I mentioned him in my first letter.) Martha is nine and Sylvie is eleven. Georgie is five and full of questions just like Frank. Mrs. McMaster doesn't like dirt and sometimes she speaks quite harshly to me especially when I make silly mistakes. She means well and I think maybe that's the important thing. Mr. McMaster seems a bit on the grumpy side, but he works in the woods all day and I scarcely see him outside of mealtime.

I must go for now. Georgie will soon come looking for me. He likes me to rock him in the evening before bedtime. Mrs. McMaster says he falls asleep much faster after being rocked. I miss you all very much.

Love, Lark

Staring down at the folded stationery, I tried to imagine how everyone's face would light up when they read my letter. I addressed the envelope, licked a stamp, and gave it to Mrs. McMaster to post. I watched her walk in the direction of the post office with the letter in her hand. I only wished I could make myself small enough to fit into the envelope and mail myself back home.

Tuesdays and Fridays, Mrs. McMaster would send Brock to the kitchen for lunch before he set back out again for Crawfordville with the mail. There were two post offices in Upper Springdale and Brock delivered mail to both of them. The post office at Mrs. McMaster's was the last one on his route. Mrs. McMaster said offering him some food before he headed back was the least she could do. I would cut cold meat and thick slices of bread spread with butter (molasses whenever he asked for it), and a cup of tea. He'd sit slightly bent forward, drawing the hot tea through his lips. "A fine cup of tea, little missy," he'd say after taking that first sip.

Brock Cameron was a tall man and thin as a whip handle. There wasn't a spare bit of fat to be found on his bones. You could almost imagine that a real strong wind might blow him away if he wasn't fastened down to something. Being skinny did little to affect his appetite. I have never seen anyone eat as much as he, not even Mr. McMaster. Some days, Georgie would sit at the table while Brock devoured his lunch.

"Give me some lassy bread, Lark," Georgie would say to me. He'd sit beside Brock Cameron eating his bread and molasses like it was a piece of chocolate cake.

"I got me a shadow," Brock said one day.

"I got me a shadow," Georgie repeated as he mimicked Brock's movements. It was most comical to watch.

"I believe you're a mite taller than you were the other day," Brock said to him between mouthfuls of food. It was the last Friday of my trial. With only three days to go, I could hardly wait.

"Do you really think so?" Georgie asked, beaming a smile up a Brock.

Brock placed his hand above Georgie's head and studied it for a while. "Why, if you aren't a speck taller, then I'm as blind as a bat."

"Did you hear that, Lark? I grew!" squealed Georgie, jumping up from the table. He raced out of the kitchen singing, "I grew…I grew…I grew."

"He's quite the lad," Brock said with a grin.

"It's too bad a few other people around this house didn't feel the same," I said, thinking out loud.

"Don't be too hard," said Brock. "This family's been through a lot." Brock was right, but knowing that didn't change the situation.

"Were they happy before Mrs. McMaster died?"

"The happiest, from what I hear," said Brock, setting his teacup down. "But they say after Dorothy died a black cloud settled over the house—cursed it or something. George Stanley has scarcely cracked a smile in all these years. Mrs. McMaster is scared she's not going to measure up to Dorothy's standards. Dorothy was a gentle soul—big-hearted. The way she was with the children, it would make you want to cry, it would, the patience she had. At least that's what people tell me."

I tried to imagine happier times, the house filled with laughter and love. It wasn't easy.

"Do you think the cloud will ever leave?"

"For a time, I thought no," said Brock Cameron. "But now I'm not so sure. What this house is in need of is change. And I'm beginning to see some changes in the last couple of weeks, missy. Good changes. And good changes don't often come along."

"You mean the way I'm always getting into trouble?"

"Mistakes are bound to happen from time to time. No one's perfect," he chuckled. I had confided a few of my mishaps to Brock last week. "It's the atmosphere here. Mrs. McMaster isn't quite so surly, and little George doesn't stand around afraid to speak." I wasn't so sure if what he'd said about Mrs. McMaster was right but little George did seem happier—when he wasn't being growled at, that is.

Brock smiled and quietly finished his tea. "A hearty thanks, missy, for the food and all," he said before leaving. But for some strange reason it felt as though I was the one who should be thanking him.

CHAPTER SEVENTEEN

"WHATCHA DOING NOW, LARK?" ASKED GEORGIE.

"Washing your dirty old shirts." It was Monday morning and the sun was shining. My trial period was nearly over and I couldn't have been happier.

He peeked down into the washtub and broke a soap bubble with his finger.

"Can I help?"

"I don't see why not."

I placed the soap in his hand and helped him rub it against the scrub board. It slid easily against the glass ribs. When the soap bar skidded from his fingers and into the washtub, we giggled. We chased the soap about the washtub. Each time I felt it beneath my fingertips it would slip from my grasp. Finally, Georgie pulled it from the water.

"You got it, Georgie! There, now jump from that," I said, setting the soap into the dish. Georgie giggled.

"What's the matter?" I asked, eyeing him with surprise. "Don't you think the soap will listen?"

He looked at me wide-eyed. I hoped I hadn't frightened him with my silly talk.

"It's scrub time now," I said. Pulling a brown shirt from the water, I gave it a good scuffing against the scrub board. We washed every inch of it before moving to the next article.

"More soap," I said. Georgie picked the bar up. This time he rubbed it on the washboard all by himself.

"I'm doing a good job, aren't I, Lark?" he said, beaming a wide smile.

"A fine job," I agreed. His eyes lit up like stars in the night sky. When the soap slipped from his hand like a greased pig, we both scrambled to catch it. Up in the air it flew. Then plop! It skidded across the kitchen floor.

"Are you ready to wring out the clothes?" Mrs. McMaster asked, barging into the kitchen at that exact moment. I held my hand up to stop her from coming any closer.

"Mrs. McMaster...No!"

It was too late. Her one foot slid out from under her as she slipped on the soapy floor.

"Lark!" she squealed. She managed to grab hold of a chair to steady herself but knocked it over in the process. It fell against the scrub board. Water splashed onto the floor. She made another step, nearly slipping. Georgie and I looked at each other with dread. I hurried toward the soap, trying to avert the impending disaster. Georgie hopped off to the corner of the kitchen. I made some steps forward, but the floor was slipperier than I thought. I grabbed for the soap, feeling it beneath in my fingers. Before I could stop, my feet went out from under me. I slammed into the washtub, landing hard on the floor. Water sloshed over me and across the floor. Placing a hand to her chest, Mrs. McMaster took in a few deep breaths moments before a shower of words rained down upon me.

"Are you trying to break my neck? Why, a fall to the floor at my age would upset one's constitution for an entire week. Who would sort the mail or run this household if I were to be laid up?"

"I'm sorry, ma'am. George and I...I was helping George," I said, looking down at the soap in my hands. My dress was completely soaked. Water dripped from my hair.

"Helping George, you say! I hardly hired George, now did I?"

"No, ma'am." I braced myself for what was to come. Surely, I was the sorriest excuse for a hired girl there ever was.

"Then kindly do your own work, Lark! That's why you're here. If George is in your way I'll have him removed. He has no business being in the kitchen while you're working. He knows that."

I stood up, gingerly choosing my steps, my wet dress hanging heavy against my legs. Why, oh why did these catastrophes keep happening? I wasn't usually clumsy, but ever since I'd arrived here it had been one disaster after another.

Mrs. McMaster's upper lip quivered as she turned toward Georgie. "You're to stay away from Lark while she's working, George McMaster. Do you hear me? For goodness' sake, you're more of a hindrance than anything. Why can't you stay out of the way?"

Georgie planted his feet on the floor. "But I was helping Lark!" he cried.

"He can sit on a chair if he wants," I offered hopefully, although I hardly thought she'd take me seriously, standing there with water dripping everywhere.

"George can entertain himself. Whatever do you think he did before you came along?"

Poor Georgie, this big old house to roam around in and no one to talk to all day long. I couldn't imagine how lonely it must be for him.

"Now, go play in your room or outside. Surely you can stay your way out of trouble." She grabbed Georgie by the shirt collar and marched him toward the back door. Tears welled up in his eyes. He looked as though he'd lost his only friend in the world. I couldn't stand it. I had to say something.

"But, Mrs. McMaster, there's truly nothing for Georgie to do here all by himself while his sisters are in school. You're always busy and there's only me to talk in this big old lonely house. The days are long, so very long for a five-year-old."

Mrs. McMaster spun around on her heels. The expression on her face told me I had no business butting into family matters.

"I'll kindly thank you to do your work, Lark Harnish, and keep your opinions to yourself. And for goodness' sake, change your dress and clean this mess up. There's work to be done. You look ridiculous."

"But I can't, ma'am...I don't mean to be disrespectful, really I don't."

She let out a grunt. Still, I continued. Surely, I could make her understand.

"Little George has nothing to do all day long. He just came out to keep me company. He's really no trouble at all. I'm used to being around young children. I don't mind him being here in the least. You have to know how to talk to them, Mrs. McMaster, or they grow up and get into all kinds of trouble."

Mrs. McMaster's face was the colour of the morning sky before a big rain but I didn't stop talking.

"There's a lad in Crawfordville who got into scads of trouble because no one in his family would give him the time of day. He ran away and no one ever heard from him again. Some folks say he stole away on a train and went to Ontario and got murdered, and others think he ended up in prison."

Mrs. McMaster towered before me.

"Are...you...quite...finished?" she asked, squeezing the question out from between her clenched teeth.

"Yes, ma'am." I was rambling on far too much. I knew that. But once I got started I couldn't get stopped. Mama always said I had more opinions than most regular folks. But sometimes you've got to stand up for what you believe in, regardless of the consequences. I was tired of the way little George was treated by the adults in this house. It just wasn't right. Where were all the hugs and kisses? Where were the smiles, the laughs? Where were the speeches about how clever a lad he was? My Grandmother Harnish brags all of us up, passing out hugs and kisses like they are going out of style.

Mrs. McMaster continued to look at me. I didn't know what else to say. It was too late to try and smooth things over now. My fate was sealed. I could see it in her eyes.

CHAPTER EIGHTEEN

THE CLOCK IN THE HALLWAY STRUCK THE HALF HOUR, INTERRUPTING Mrs. McMaster before she had time to speak. The vibration echoed throughout the house. When I looked about, Georgie was nowhere to be seen. I couldn't much blame him.

"Well, well, I'd say that was quite the little speech, Lark Harnish, and you on the last day of your trial."

Her words came out like raindrops splattering on a tin roof. There was no doubt in my mind that a downpour would come at any moment. I knew better than to interrupt. I'd had my say. Now it was her turn. She made a tutting sound, shaking her head back and forth. I silently screamed for the downpour to arrive, to have it be over and done with.

"I can see this isn't working. I've tried to be patient, Lark Harnish. Goodness only knows I've given you that much." Her fingers were locked together as she circled around me. "Young people need to be given a chance. I said so to George Stanley just the other day. But now this...I daresay you've been a challenge right from day one. Is it me? Have I been unreasonable?" She stopped directly in front of me.

"No, ma'am," I whispered, shaking my head. I was a miserable excuse for a hired girl. I'd made more than my share of mistakes. To top things off, I couldn't keep my opinions to myself.

"Perhaps if you were older..."

She looked about, shaking her head. The kitchen was a disaster, with water and soap bubbles all about. The wash would never be out before Bertha Gray's. The cucumbers we'd picked last night and covered in brine were still waiting to be made into pickles.

"Vera Wright's girl is looking for work. I heard so just the other day. She's older, more experienced..."

My head was hanging low. I waited for her to say more, but what more was there to say? I was sure Vera Wright's daughter would make a better hired girl.

I dragged myself up the stairs and put on a new dress. I helped Mrs. McMaster clean the kitchen and then we finished the wash. Neither of us spoke. I couldn't think of anything to say. Nothing would make the situation better. Already, I could see the disappointment in Mama's eyes when I showed up back home. Worse yet, I could forget about anyone else hiring me, not when word got out that Mrs. McMaster had let me go and exactly why. Bertha Gray would have a field day spreading *that* story around.

We set the wash basket down on the grass between us. The sun peeked out through a mass of grey clouds. There was a quiet rumble of thunder in the distance. I hoped the storm clouds wouldn't head our way.

"The day started out sunny enough," said Mrs. McMaster quietly. She looked toward the sky. "Although I daresay our weather has been so changeable lately."

Rain on washday would simply be the icing on the cake. I handed Mrs. McMaster one of Mr. McMaster's work shirts. For once, I didn't want to talk.

"I'll settle up with you before Brock Cameron arrives tomorrow with a more than generous wage," said Mrs. McMaster. "I won't have it said I shorted you in any way. Don't worry about the broken china. It was old anyway."

I reached into the basket, trying hard to swallow the lump that was growing in my throat. Another rumble sounded in the distance. Mrs. McMaster paid no attention but continued to set the clothes out. Tomorrow was mail day. I would leave with Brock Cameron. She would never have to set eyes on me again.

"Lark," she said, clearing her throat. She no longer sounded angry, although I might have preferred it if she had. I stopped. I couldn't look at her. Nothing she had to say would make me feel better. "Sometimes we expect too much from ourselves... and others. But you mustn't let this experience discourage you. Perhaps when you're older, you'll—"

The back door slammed. Georgie came running toward us yelling, "Fire! Fire!"

"Fire? Where?" Mrs. McMaster dropped the dress she had in her hands. "What the devil have you done now, George? If you've set the house on fire—"

We ran for the house, to see what had happened.

"No. Outside...I saw the smoke from upstairs."

Changing directions, we raced out to the end of the pole fence and looked toward the sky.

"I don't see a thing," said Mrs. McMaster as she scanned the treeline. She turned toward Georgie. "What have I told you about making up stories?" A long rumble of thunder answered her question.

"I'm not making up stories! I saw it from upstairs...You believe me, don't you, Lark?"

"My word, where are you off to, Lark Harnish?" asked Mrs. McMaster as I suddenly sprinted past her. There was no time to spare. I prayed Georgie had been mistaken as I raced into the house and up the stairs.

"Lark Harnish, you sound like an old horse clomping up those steps, now you come back down here this minute!" Mrs. McMaster's voice echoed up from the kitchen below, but I didn't stop. She'd be angry with me again, but what was the worst thing she could do? I'd already been fired.

"What's this world coming to? Everyone in this house does exactly as they please. ...Now, you stay here in the kitchen and stop making up stories, George McMaster...Upsetting my constitution like this...and twice in one day," she grumbled as she marched up the stairs. "Now Lark, come down from there this minute. I'm afraid you fell for one of George's tricks." She reached the upstairs window, where I stood searching for signs of smoke.

"Not that window," cried little George, suddenly standing in the hallway in front of his bedroom, "this one!" I swung around and nearly bumped into Mrs. McMaster. We hurried across the hallway to George's room. He was jumping up and down. "See?" he said, pointing out the window. "I didn't make anything up"

Thin wisps of gray smoke spiralled up through the treetops. Desperation formed a rock in the pit of my stomach. We hadn't had rain for over a week, and there was no guarantee we'd get much now; a fire might spread quickly. What would we do?

"It must have been a lightning strike. Go ring the bell out in the pasture!" cried Mrs. McMaster. "Ring it as long as you dare. The men will come out of the woods. Help will come from all over."

I raced to where the bell sat high in the air at the top of a pole. A thick braided rope was fastened to it. I loosened it and pulled. The noise echoed across the field, high above the tree-tops. I pulled on it, again and again. Would help come as Mrs. McMaster had predicted? As I raced back toward the house, I knew one thing for certain. I wasn't about to wait and find out.

CHAPTER NINETEEN

"I HOPE SOMEONE SOON GETS HERE," MRS. MCMASTER SAID, PACING BACK and forth across the kitchen floor.

"We can't just stand here and do nothing," I said. "The fire could spread before the men make it out of the woods."

"We did our part by ringing the bell. All we can do is wait," said Mrs. McMaster. But I knew there had to be something more we could do.

"Maybe we can put it out ourselves," I said, hurrying past her.

"Put it out ourselves? What can we do—an old woman and two children? No, I'm afraid we'll have to wait for the men. That makes the most sense. They'll bring shovels and picks, tools to fight fire that we can't possibly manage. We must be realistic in these situations and keep a level head. We can make food—in case it's needed, I mean. All disasters call for food."

"We can do more than make food—and it's not a disaster, not yet at least." Mrs. McMaster wouldn't like me talking up to her, but I didn't care. She was wrong; disasters call for action. "Right now, it doesn't look like much smoke. Maybe the fire is small. And if the lightning hit the ground, it might even burn itself out, but we can't take any chances." I thought for a few moments. "I know!" I said. "Maybe I can beat it out with some blankets."

"Do you really think?" Hope sparked in Mrs. McMaster's voice.

"I have to try at least."

Last spring Mr. Dickson had burned off the field behind his house. The fire started to get away from him, creeping dangerously close to his house. Mama and I helped him beat it out with wool blankets. Maybe I could do the same with this fire, or at least slow it down until help arrived.

Mrs. McMaster hurried down the hallway and opened a trunk in her bedroom. A grey wool blanket was lying on top. "It's an old one, but it's heavy."

The smell of mothballs was strong. I gathered it in my arms and ran out to the porch. Mrs. McMaster was close at my heels.

"When help comes, I'll send them your way," she said. "And in the meantime, you be careful, Lark Harnish. Don't take any foolish chances, do you hear me? Fire is not something to play with. We could end up being burned out."

The wooded area where we'd seen the smoke was on the other side of the pasture. I raced toward the fence, hoping I'd locate the fire quickly. I was getting ready to crawl beneath it when Charlie whinnied at me. I looked at him. I knew then what to do.

"Come, Charlie. Come boy," I called. Pulling out some thick blades of fresh grass, I tried to entice him over to the gate. He snorted and shook his head. "Please, Charlie," I begged. "I need your help." Head held high, he trotted toward me this time. His thick lips began to flap and he soon picked the grass off my open palm. I patted his neck, urging him to come closer.

Climbing the pole fence, I attempted to scramble onto his back, but he wanted no part of it.

"Please, Charlie," I begged again. "There's a fire. I need the help of a smart horse like you. Please don't let me down."

This time Charlie stood still and I slid onto his broad back. I wrapped my hand around his mane the same way I used to with Jim whenever I went for a ride. With the blanket resting safely across my lap, we took off across the pasture.

"Hurry, Charlie, hurry," I urged, pushing my heels into his sides. With a quick jump, he kicked up his big hind feet and began to run like a spring colt. I held on tight, trying not to fall. He wasn't a swift horse, but he'd get me there quicker than my own two legs. Nearing the far side of the pasture, I pulled back on Charlie's mane and let out a soft "whoa." He whinnied and came to a stop. I patted his neck. "Good boy, Charlie. Good boy."

Whiffs of smoke reached my nostrils. There was no time to waste. Throwing the wool blanket onto the ground, I slid down off Charlie's back. Crawling beneath the fence, I pushed my way through the barrier of bushes in front of me, holding fast to the blanket. But which way to turn? I couldn't see a single flame or wisp of smoke.

There came another long rumble of thunder in the distance and I glanced toward the darkening sky. Frantically, I searched about for signs of a fire but saw nothing. Behind me Charlie whinnied. Another whiff of smoke reached me. Clutching the blanket in my arms, I made my way to a small clearing. Waves of relief flowed through me. I'd found it!

Grey smoke billowed up from a toppled tree that had snapped in two. The bark was ripped and split. Mrs. McMaster had been right. It was a lightning strike. I couldn't see any flames, but a fire could be smouldering inside the tree, waiting to ignite. The smoke had to be coming from somewhere. I might be able to smother it with the blanket before that happened.

I hurried closer, but before I reached the tree, my feet got tangled in the blanket and I stumbled. Crying out, I fell into the grass and sticks. A sharp pain hit me in my chest. I tried to get up but couldn't move as I fought to get air into my lungs. Smoke continued to rise up from the tree stump, but I was still unable to move. I had to get up off the ground and start beating the fire before the stump ignited.

Charlie's much welcomed whinny reminded me that I wasn't completely alone. I managed to sit up. Taking in some slow breaths, the fear in me began to dwindle. Gradually, I made it to my feet. As smoke continued to roll from the stricken tree, I hurried toward it and unrolled the blanket.

Red glowing embers pulsing deep in the tree, gently ignited. The flames were small, but if the wind came up that could quickly change. Smoke continued to rise. Clutching the wool blanket, I beat at the flames, but my arms soon tired. The blanket was too big for me to handle on my own. Maybe if I folded it I could snuff out the flames, or at least slow them down until help arrived. Doubling it into a manageable size, I beat at the tree stump with every ounce of strength in me—over and over—but the flames refused to shrink. A spray of sparks sputtered up in the air. Tiny embers landed in the grass and leaves near my feet. Smoke quickly curled up from the ground. I'd made things worse. The fire began to lick the dry blades of grass as tiny flames inched across the ground.

My arms begging for a rest, I dropped the blanket and began stepping on the flames. No sooner would I get them out than more would spring up. The flames grew warm against my toes as I continued to stomp at the ground. Eventually the flames disappeared into the blackened earth. With no time to waste, I turned back toward the smouldering stump. Checking quickly over my shoulder, I hoped help was on the way, but I saw no one. Again, Charlie whinnied, telling me to hurry. Lifting the blanket, I went back to beating the tree stump, hoping to smother the flames. My arms quickly turned to rubber. Tears pressed against my throat. Determination doesn't count for much if you're too tired to move a muscle. I sat down to try and catch my breath. This was much harder than I'd thought.

Something crackled in the woods behind me. Another crack and I called out, "Who is it? Who's there?" I'd overheard Firth and Trent talking about a bear Firth had seen beneath some wild apple trees last week. There was an apple tree on this side of the fence. I'd seen it when I slid down off of Charlie's back. My heart was drumming in my chest. My mind raced, going through the things I knew about bears and how best to avoid them. Climbing a tree was out since they were excellent climbers. They are fast, so I knew I couldn't outrun it. But then I remembered Papa once saying that if you ever cross paths with a bear, your best defence is to play dead. Acting quickly, I stretched out on the ground, hoping whatever it was it would pass me by. Surely I wasn't a big enough morsel for a hungry bear.

The ground beneath me vibrated as whatever it was came closer. I squeezed my eyes shut and waited, my heart thrashing loudly. What kind of noise did a bear make? I tried not to breathe as it closed in on me. Fear gripped me as I lay there waiting. The soft sound of footsteps stopped not far from where I lay. I was more afraid than I'd ever been in my life. My trepidation grew as I waited for whatever it was to pass by. Would it bite into me, gnaw on my body despite my pretending to be dead, or would it walk right on by?

When I could stand it no longer, I opened one eye and took a tiny peek, and when I saw what it was, I screamed like I'd never screamed before.

CHAPTER TWENTY

"LARK HARNISH, WOULD YOU KINDLY STOP THAT INCESSANT BLARING. You'll deafen me." Mrs. McMaster stood but a few inches from me, staring down into my face, her hands cupped over her ears.

"Mrs. McMaster—what are you doing here?" I sat up quickly. I was so relieved not to be staring into the beady brown eyes of a bear that I could have hugged her.

"Doing here? I couldn't very well stay at the house with a fire burning somewhere on our property. And for goodness' sake, get yourself up off the ground. You're supposed to be fighting fire, not stretched out taking a nap."

"I thought you were a bear," I said. For once I didn't mind her disapproval.

"A bear?" Mrs. McMaster huffed, as if that suggestion was ridiculous.

"I...I was playing dead," I said, trying to explain. It all sounded silly now. The only real danger I'd been facing was the danger of a tongue-lashing from Mrs. McMaster.

"And in the meantime, a fire rages behind you. Now stop talking and do something constructive, like putting it out," she said. I looked over my shoulder. Mrs. McMaster was right. The flames had gotten bigger.

There came more rustling through the bushes and then little George emerged.

"Lark!" he squealed, making his way toward me. He was struggling with a water container, dragging it behind him with both hands. He stopped not far from the smouldering stump.

"Grandmother, you forgot the water," he said, panting. Mrs. McMaster grabbed my outstretched arm and helped me to my feet. Georgie ran over and hugged fast to my waist.

"Step back," said Mrs. McMaster to little George. "There's work to be done. I told you before we left home, you were to stay well out of the way." A sad look came over Georgie's face, but he listened to what his grandmother had to say.

I grabbed the water and hurried toward the smoking stump.

"No, wait. There's not enough to put it out. Bring the water here. We'll stretch out the blanket." She quickly wetted it with the water from the container. "The wool will soak up the water and help suffocate the flames."

I was glad she'd forgotten her plan to stay home and make food as we grabbed both ends of the blanket. If we worked together, we might just get it out before it had time to spread.

"We won't leave the blanket there too long," she said as we lowered it over the flames. "It might catch fire if we do." I did as Mrs. McMaster instructed. "Now be careful not to beat too hard, Lark Harnish. You'll send the sparks flying."

"Yes, Mrs. McMaster," I said. I could have told her I'd already discovered that. When little George ran over and grabbed my end of the blanket, Mrs. McMaster quickly intervened.

"Little George, you stay out of the way. We can do this without you."

Georgie moaned. "I want to help too," he said.

"Why, you did help," I said. "You brought the water to us, and an important part that was." That put the smile back on his face.

Finally, the smoke was no longer rolling up. We removed the blanket. The flames were gone. The tree stump was burnt black. The blanket was badly scorched, but the water had kept it from burning up.

"We did it, Mrs. McMaster!" I said. "We did it all on our own without the men."

"Yes well, it seems this was indeed within our capabilities," she said. Her smudged hand left a black streak across her cheek as she pulled a lock of hair off her forehead. The more I studied her face, the funnier it seemed. I started to laugh.

"What's so funny?" she demanded. Mrs. McMaster looked as though she were sporting a black eye.

"Your face," I said, pointing. "There's a black streak." She really was a sorry-looking sight.

"*My* face? I should think you'd want to check in a mirror yourself. Why, you look like you rolled in an ashpan," she said. I stopped laughing and for a second, we stood staring at one another. Then suddenly we were both laughing, still holding fast to the charred wool blanket. Behind us, Charlie whinnied.

"Charlie's laughing too," said Georgie, his eyes shining, and we laughed again. But what happened next caused us to become quite serious. It was Mr. McMaster scrabbling his way through the undergrowth with Trent and Firth close behind. He was carrying a double-bladed axe; Firth and Trent each had a shovel.

"What's all this?" he asked, sending the three of us a questioning look. "We heard the bell and came out, but there was no one at the house. Just Charlie standing out here pawing the ground. Then we saw the smoke."

I was sure we were a pitiful sight to behold, but I didn't care.

"Lightning," explained Mrs. McMaster.

"We heard it rumbling this morning," said Trent.

"It hit the tree," continued Mrs. McMaster. "But thankfully, with Lark's quick actions, we got it out."

Mr. McMaster had an odd expression on his face. He looked at me and nodded. It was difficult to tell what he was thinking.

"Lark saves the day, by the looks of it," said Trent patting my shoulder.

"We worked together," I said, smiling at Mrs. McMaster. "And Georgie did his part, too."

Mr. McMaster looked at little George but said nothing.

Firth took his shovel and went over to examine the burned tree. "It could be burning in the roots," he said. "I've seen fires start up again." He started digging near the tree with his shovel, upturning the soil, looking for any signs of fire. Trent and Mr. McMaster joined in. Mr. McMaster stopped, his axe in mid-swing.

"No need to stay. Go home and get cleaned up. You look a fright," he told his mother. "We'll take it from here."

Gathering up what was left of the blanket, we walked back to where Charlie was waiting by the fence.

"It's out, Charlie. The fire is out," I said. He brought his head down to meet me, his lips flapping. "We couldn't have done it without your help. Thank you...thank you for getting me here so quickly." Charlie whinnied softly and brought his head down toward little George.

"Good old Charlie," said Georgie, patting his nose.

"He still has plenty of spirit left in him," I said. "Are you ready to go home?" I was too tired to care that I no longer had a job with the McMasters.

I helped Georgie scramble up the fence and onto Charlie's back before climbing on myself. Mrs. McMaster was heading toward the back gate, carrying what was left of the wool blanket. She opened it and stepped through, fastening it behind her. I remembered then she wasn't fond of horses. Perhaps she'd have a change of heart, seeing how Charlie had been a big help today.

I grabbed Charlie's mane and rubbed his neck gently. "Hang on tight," I told little George. He twined his fingers around the hair on Charlie's thick brown mane. We trotted across the pasture, tired but satisfied.

When we made it back to the house, there were people in the dooryard. Georgie and I climbed the fence and jumped down on the other side. Mrs. McMaster had said the neighbours would come if I range the bell.

"There was a fire, but we put it out," I explained and thanked them for coming. As I took Georgie inside, the thunder rumbled and a few drops of rain began to fall.

To my surprise, Bertha Gray was sitting at the kitchen table. She looked at me and scowled. "My, my, you're a mess, Lark Harnish," she said.

I quickly told her about the fire, then added, "Thank you for the concern. I'll tell Mrs. McMaster you came by." All I could think about was getting cleaned up. But she wouldn't leave.

"It's not your place to fight fire, Lark Harnish. You're the hired girl, not a field hand." She was looking at me as though I'd done something horribly wrong.

Mrs. McMaster came into the kitchen just then. "Just be glad this girl was here," she said.

"Nadine, look at you," said Bertha as she scrutinized Mrs. McMaster, with soot smudged on her face and her hair a horrible mess. "My word, I'd never have guessed you'd be influenced by a"—she glared at me—"hired girl of all people. Why, if Dorothy were here…"

"Well, Dorothy is not here," Mrs. McMaster said coldly. Bertha glared at little George as if he were to blame. "But Lark is, and thankfully so. Now, I thank you very much for coming. If you'll excuse me, I need to change."

Bertha Gray let out a grunt as she got up from the chair. When the porch door closed, Mrs. McMaster turned toward me.

"Do not go far. I'm going to get cleaned up and then I'll need to have a word with you," she said with a stoic face. "Now, go make yourself presentable."

"Yes, ma'am," I answered quietly.

I washed my face and hands and hurried upstairs to change. By the time I came back down, Mrs. McMaster was in the kitchen. We looked at each other and for a moment neither of us seemed to know what to say. I thought about what to tell Mama when I got home, how best to explain it all, as I waited for Mrs. McMaster to speak.

Chapter Twenty-One

Dear Mama,

My trial period is finally over and Mrs. McMaster has asked me to stay on. I couldn't be happier. I'm getting along well with the children here and I believe I'm even growing on Mrs. McMaster.

I was happy to hear that Fluffy brought out three kittens, but whatever will you do with them all? Tell Midge and Frank not to handle them too much or it'll stunt their growth.

There's a hint of autumn in the air these days, and the leaves are beginning to change. Shades of red and orange peek out at me from across the pasture. I can see them from my bedroom window. There are many trees in the yard here, maple and oak and birch. I'm sure they will put on a handsome show in the weeks ahead. How I'd love to see a beech tree, but sadly there are none in the yard.

Mrs. McMaster says she is expecting a heavy frost any time now. Most everything has been cleaned out of the garden. One of these days, Trent and Firth will help Mr. McMaster dig the potatoes. Like Papa used to say, there's nothing like a pot full of new potatoes with Sunday dinner.

The day is getting late and I must go rock Georgie before bedtime. Write to me soon with all your news. I miss you all so very much.

Love, Lark

One afternoon in mid-October, I was scrubbing the upstairs hallway with a good deal of satisfaction in my heart. Things had been going quite well for me, and it had been a long time since Mrs. McMaster had found reason to scold me for anything. Since the fire, her behaviour toward me seemed to have changed, and she didn't speak so sharply whenever I did have a mishap.

Pulling the bucket along as I scrubbed, I made my way down the long corridor. I looked up at the portrait of young Mrs. McMaster. I couldn't help thinking how sad she'd be if she knew how the household had changed. From below me, I could hear Mrs. McMaster pacing along the floor. I'd been with the family going on two months and was getting used to their way of doing things, even when their way was totally different from what Mama taught me. Mrs. McMaster said I needed to adapt more flexibility into my routine, which sounded comical coming from her of all people. I was learning that the amusing things she said were most times not intended to be funny at all.

Along with there being a time to be quiet, I had figured out that there is also a time to refrain from laughing. I had plenty more to learn and, despite her impatience, Mrs. McMaster was usually quite good at explaining how to do things. Which probably had to do with her once having taught school before she became Mrs. McMaster. Although she was getting used to me being about, and even managed a slight smile on several occasions, it was a totally different story with Mr. McMaster. I was beginning to wonder if there could possibly be anything inside that hard, shrivelled heart of his to smile about.

That particular morning in October as I was scrubbing the hallway floor, I considered how to get into Sylvie's good graces. Perhaps I could find something we might have in common. It wasn't an easy thing, since Sylvie didn't seem to have many interests. She didn't collect anything, nor did she appear to like the farm animals. She spent much of her time in her room reading books. Occasionally Rebecca O'Reily would come by to visit and I'd sometimes see them in the dooryard, but when Rebecca wasn't there Sylvie only played outside when her grandmother ordered her to. I'd made fast friends with Martha and Georgie, but not so with Sylvie. In many ways, she reminded me of her father.

As I puzzled over some way to befriend Sylvie, Mrs. McMaster called for me. "Lark...Lark Harnish! Come here at once!" There was urgency in her voice. Dropping my scrub brush, I hurried to see what I had done wrong this time.

"Yes, Mrs. McMaster?" When I reached the bottom of the stairs, she stopped pacing the floor.

"Mrs. Walker was in here a few weeks back with a small parcel to post. Do you remember?"

"Yes, ma'am." It had been late in the day and the post office had only just closed when Mrs. Walker came rushing in through the porch. She asked Mrs. McMaster if she'd mind opening the post office back up again.

Worry was stretched across Mrs. McMaster's face as she began to pace the floor again.

"What's wrong, Mrs. McMaster? Is there something I can do?"

She sighed and called for the children to come immediately. I couldn't imagine what she wanted of them. When they were all present, she began. Her voice was a mixture of anger and concern.

"It has been brought to my attention that a parcel mailed from here a few weeks back never reached its destination. In fact, it seems it never left this house." I gulped, knowing how serious this could be for Mrs. McMaster. The children stood wide-eyed in front of their grandmother. "I want to know if someone here has been in the post office."

The children all promised, again and again, that they hadn't been anywhere near the parcels and letters, but Mrs. McMaster continued to quiz them. At one point, Martha broke out in tears.

"If you've done nothing wrong, then you've nothing to worry about," Mrs. McMaster said as Martha wiped her eyes. "But heaven help any of you if you're not telling the truth." She angrily searched their faces. "I will *not* abide lie telling in this house."

How could a parcel go missing under Mrs. McMaster's vigilant eye? This whole thing had me baffled. She was always so careful. Besides, no one was allowed in the post office unless she was present.

"I don't understand it," she said, clearly shaken. "The parcel came through here but didn't arrive in Crawfordville. How can that be? I've been racking my brain. Trying to think of some explanation. Things don't just disappear."

"Perhaps it fell out of Brock's mailbag?" I suggested.

"I doubt that very much," said Mrs. McMaster, "although I could ask him if there were any incidences of the bag being dropped. I clearly remember putting the parcel in with the out-going mail. Most parcels aren't that small, so it stuck in my mind, and then Mrs. Walker blustering in the way she did. Perhaps I was distracted."

I looked down at little George, suddenly remembering the day I'd caught him racing from the post office. That was over a month ago. Mrs. Walker had only just mailed her parcel two weeks back. But then a fearful thought wiggled into my head. What if that was not the only time little George had gone into the post office? He spent plenty of time by himself each day with nothing to do. I can only image how horrible that must be for a five-year-old. Had his curiosity about the "forbidden room" got-ten the best of him? Had he snuck into the post office, seen the little parcel, and become overcome with temptation?

But then Sylvie spoke up. "Lark let Georgie into the post office one day." The shock of what she'd said caught me off guard. I looked at her, my mouth gaped open. I couldn't believe it.

"Is this so?" I studied Mrs. McMaster's face as she waited for me to say something. But I had nothing to say in my own defence. I should have told her I caught little George coming out of the post office that day. Except he'd been so afraid of landing in trouble. He swore he hadn't touched anything, so I promised him his grandmother would never have to know. He'd been curious, and he hadn't done any harm.

"Is this a fact, Lark? Answer me," said Mrs. McMaster forcefully. Her jaw was stiff and her eyes dark with anger. How could I answer truthfully without landing Georgie in a whole lot of trouble? Truth is important, but so is friendship, and friends don't tattle on one another, not even to keep themselves out of trouble. I looked at Sylvie, standing before her grandmother with her arms folded in front of her. She was smirking.

"I...well...it's just that..." No sensible explanation formed in my mind.

"This is totally unacceptable, Lark Harnish. Your trial period might be over, but that does *not* give you an excuse to do whatever you want in this house."

"Her trial period wasn't even over when *that* happened," injected Sylvie, holding her head high. I tried to speak for myself, but Mrs. McMaster stopped me.

"Silence," she barked. "I have maintained from the start that the post office was off limits. A fact that everyone here is well aware of. Why did you not report this to me immediately?"

"George was afraid...I didn't see the harm."

"You didn't see that harm? *You*?" said Mrs. McMaster as if she couldn't believe what she was hearing.

"I'm so sorry, Mrs. McMaster." But I knew that wouldn't help. It was too late to change the past.

"Sorry seems to be your excuse for everything, Lark Harnish, and it's getting a little old." She sighed. "George Stanley will not be pleased at all. He hardly welcomed the idea of having the post office in the house in the first place. I told him it would be fine, but now this." She held her hand to her forehead. "I'm going to lie down for a bit. I have a splitting headache. I will deal with this later when I've had time to think. Now, outside with you," she said to the children, waving them on. "Lark, finish scrubbing the floor and get on with the rest of your chores. I will figure out a reasonable punishment. But in the meantime, that doesn't bring Mrs. Walker's parcel back."

Mrs. McMaster marched off and the house became unusually quiet. "You heard Grandmother...Now come on, Georgie and Martha," said Sylvie, flashing me an amused look. None of this made sense. How could Sylvie possibly know that Georgie had been in the post office? He must have told her. But why had he confided in Sylvie, of all people?

The moment Mrs. McMaster disappeared down the hallway, little George charged toward me angrily, pushing me with both of his hands. I stumbled backward.

"What did you do that for?" I asked, perplexed by his actions.

"You promised you wouldn't tell, Lark," he said with hurt in his eyes.

"Tell? I didn't tell anyone...well, only Mama...but that was in a letter. She doesn't even know your grandmother."

I stopped suddenly and looked at Sylvie as I entertained the only answer there was. I'd put the letter in an envelope after I wrote it, but hadn't sealed it right away. But surely, she wouldn't have...except there *was* no other explanation. A strange look crept across Sylvie's face when I said the only thing that made sense.

"You read the letter I wrote Mama, didn't you?" The smirk she'd been sporting moments before disappeared.

I waited for her to admit what she'd done. But it seemed that wasn't to be.

"Come on, Martha and Georgie, Grandmother said we should go outside." She turned to me and added, "And you're to be scrubbing the floor."

Anger boiled inside me. All this time I'd tried to be nice to Sylvie, to show her we could be friends. Two months and nothing had worked. Not only that, she'd snuck into my room and read my private letter to Mama. I was through being nice. Being nice to Sylvie had gotten me nowhere. She was spoiled and bossy and as mean as her father, and now she'd invaded my privacy.

She started to leave and I grabbed her arm.

"Leave go of me," she said, pulling back. "I'll tell Grandmother." I let go of her arm. She looked at me with her nose in the air.

"Then while you're doing that, you can tell her you were snooping in my room and read my mail," I said.

"You have no proof of that. You wouldn't even be here if you hadn't put out that stupid fire. I heard Papa tell Grandmother that you're more trouble than you're worth." Seeing the hurt on my face, Sylvie smiled smugly. "Come on," she said to Martha and Georgie.

"No, Sylvie!" said Martha, only just now speaking up. "I saw you come out of the post office one day."

Sylvie's eyes grew wide. "I don't believe you. You're just making that up," she said. "Now, come on." She attempted to take Martha's hand.

"No, I'm not making it up," said Martha, pushing Sylvie's hand aside. "You were carrying something and you ran upstairs with it."

"Liar. You didn't see anything, because there was no one around—" Sylvie clamped her hands over her mouth as she realized what she'd said.

CHAPTER TWENTY-TWO

"I'M TELLING GRANDMOTHER YOU TOOK MRS. WALKER'S PARCEL," threatened Martha. Sylvie stood frozen as Martha walked off to find Mrs. McMaster, her eyes darting about in fear.

"No, Martha," I said, bringing her to a halt. She spun around, puzzled.

"But Lark, Sylvie—" Martha started to say.

"...had a lapse in judgement," I said, looking calmly at Sylvie. I was relieved to know the parcel had not truly gone missing, and as much as Sylvie deserved to be punished, I couldn't let that happen. I suddenly felt sorry for her. If Mama had turned bitter and cold after Papa died, maybe I'd be mean too. What Sylvie needed was understanding, not anger, but I knew her grandmother wouldn't see it that way. I dreaded the thought of what she'd do.

Sylvie was eagerly nodding. "That's right. It was a lapse," she agreed, producing a sad face. "I made a mistake, a horrible mistake."

Her sudden contrition didn't fool me, but continuing to blame her wouldn't fix the immediate problem. Somehow the parcel had to get back into the post office without Mrs. McMaster finding out what really happened.

"Now, the question is: what to do? I'm open to any and all suggestions," I said as the children huddled around me. I wasn't familiar with the post office, since Mrs. McMaster insisted she be the one to clean it. I'd only ever caught glimpses of it those times the post office was open for business.

Martha looked at her sister. "Why did you even take it?" she asked. Sylvie looked at the floor.

"Rebecca was here that afternoon. We saw Mrs. Walker come in with the parcel. She dared me."

"You do know tampering with the mail is against the law?" I said. What could she have been thinking?

"Rebecca wanted to open it, but I wouldn't let her. I was going to put it back, but there was never a good time."

"I think Sylvie should come up with a plan. It's all her fault," said Martha.

"No, Martha," I said firmly. "We'll figure something out together." Even though Sylvie hadn't once been nice to me, I didn't want her to get into trouble. Maybe if someone showed her kindness, she would stop being so nasty all the time. Besides, if the parcel finally arrived at its destination, what harm would there be? A late parcel is better than no parcel at all.

"We can tell her we found it in the barn!" came Georgie's suggestion.

"That's stupid," said Sylvie.

"Is not," Georgie insisted.

"Is too," agreed Martha.

I held up a finger, warning them not to squabble amongst themselves. We'd never come up with a solution that way.

"What if we give it to Brock? He could take it to the post office in Crawfordville for us," said Martha. I considered Martha's suggestion. I was almost sure Brock would be willing to help out if I asked. Mrs. McMaster would never have to find out. She might be so happy to learn that the parcel had mysteriously appeared at the Crawfordville post office that she wouldn't question it. I mulled that over for a bit, but decided against it. It wouldn't be right to involve Brock.

"That would be like asking Brock to lie for us," I said, "and one lie only leads to another. It could make matters worse."

"What if we put it back in the post office?" suggested Martha.

"That's stupid too. Grandmother would wonder where it suddenly came from."

"At least I thought of something," said Martha, glaring at her sister. "That's more than you're doing, Sylvie."

I thought quickly through this. "That might just work!" I said, much to Sylvie's surprise. Martha looked at her sister and pulled a face.

"The parcel is small and could easily be overlooked by someone if they were quite busy," I said, thinking out loud. "Didn't your grandmother say there's a box that holds the outgoing parcels?"

"It's on the table with some stamps and papers, next to the wall. It was piled high that day. That's where the parcel was when I took it," said Sylvie sheepishly, realizing what she'd just owned up to.

"What if we put the parcel somewhere in the post office for Grandmother to find?" said Martha.

"That's what I'm thinking too—but where? Wherever we put it, it would have to make sense. We can't set it out in the open." If only I knew more about the layout of the post office…but Sylvie was the only one who knew that. There was little George, but I very much doubted that he'd remember. I turned to Sylvie. "You've been in the post office. Where would be the best place for a parcel to get lost?"

Sylvie shrugged. "I don't know."

"Can't you be a teensy bit helpful?" I asked, suddenly annoyed. Her lack of concern irritated me. I was racking my brain to keep *her* out of trouble. The least she could do was make some suggestions. "We're trying to help you out, Sylvie, but you won't cooperate even a bit. Perhaps we shouldn't help you at all. Perhaps Martha should just tell your grandmother. Is that what you want?"

"No. Don't!" said Sylvie so loudly I thought Mrs. McMaster might hear. Our heads turned in the direction she had gone. When we saw or heard nothing, Sylvie lowered her voice and said, "Let me think." She paused for a few moments. "It's no good…I can't remember."

"Maybe close your eyes and picture the post office in your head."

For once, Sylvie took my suggestion. Suddenly she snapped her eyes open and her face lit up. "The table where the box was sitting!"

"What about it?" Martha wanted to know.

"The tablecloth goes all the way to the floor." Sylvie searched our faces, looking for us to understand. "If a small parcel got knocked out of the box and onto the floor…"

"Ah," I said, catching on. "It might get kicked underneath the tablecloth and not be seen. That's brilliant, Sylvie!"

Sylvie looked at me for the first time and smiled.

"Here's what we'll do," I said, drawing them all in close.

Later, as I was helping Mrs. McMaster prepare supper, the children came into the kitchen. Sylvie quickly put our plan into action. She volunteered to help her grandmother look for the missing parcel one last time.

"I don't see what good that will do," said Mrs. McMaster wearily. "I've turned the room upside down. It's nowhere to be seen."

"It can't do any harm. Sometimes another set of eyes will see something new," I said, eager to give her some hope of it being found. But my cheery words were met by Mrs. McMaster's glaring eyes.

"There is still the matter of you allowing little George into the post office. I haven't yet decided what to do with you *or* little George. But rest assured I'll think of something," she added tartly.

"Lark didn't let me in the post office. I went in by myself," said Georgie suddenly. "She told me to get out…I'm sorry."

"Is that so?" Mrs. McMaster looked down at Georgie, unimpressed. "I have told you all, time and again. The post office is off limits."

"I won't do it ever again. I promise," said little George, looking remorseful. "Please don't be mad. I had a lapse."

Mrs. McMaster loomed over little George, wearing a dissatisfied look.

"Very well, but if I ever hear tell of you going in there again, you'll be sorry, young man." She looked at the three of them. "That goes for all of you. Do you understand?" They nodded anxiously.

Sylvie cleared her throat. "We were going to check the post office again, Grandmother. Remember?" This time Mrs. McMaster reluctantly agreed.

I waited outside the post office with Martha and Georgie while Mrs. McMaster and Sylvie searched for the missing parcel. There was a desk near the doorway, stacked with papers and envelopes and all sorts of stationery supplies. Along one wall was a table covered with a pretty green tablecloth that went right to the floor, just as Sylvie had described. There was a wooden box on the table with a sign on the side that said *Outgoing*.

"The room is smaller than I thought," whispered Martha as Sylvie and her grandmother searched all about.

There were mail slots fastened to a wall. Each slot had the family name beneath it. I smiled, seeing one marked *Harnish*.

"I checked all these mail slots before," sighed Mrs. McMasters as she examined each one with care. Sylvie looked out at me and I nodded. It was time to put our plan in motion. Sylvie got down on her hands and knees and lifted the corner of the long tablecloth.

"It's here, Grandmother. I can see it!" she exclaimed.

Mrs. McMaster whirled around. "You found it?" she said gleefully.

"Yes, Grandmother...but I can't reach it," said Sylvie, straining. Mrs. McMasters hurriedly held up the tablecloth while Sylvie disappeared beneath table. Moments later she presented the parcel to her grandmother.

"My word, I looked under there earlier, but my back. It's stiff. I suppose I couldn't see all the way," she said, clutching the parcel. She looked down at the children, her mouth suddenly drawn tight with remorse. "And to think I thought one of you was responsible."

That night, a gentle knock came to my bedroom door. It was Sylvie looking most serious.

"About today?" she said meekly.

"Yes?" I answered, anxious to hear what she would say.

She cleared her throat. "Thank you," she mumbled quickly and then hurried away.

CHAPTER TWENTY-THREE

FALL ARRIVED EARLY, AND I FOUND MYSELF DESPERATELY LONGING FOR home. Autumn is my favourite time of year, with the breeze packed with goose bumps, and the leaves turned orange and red.

Last fall we raked leaves and set them afire. There was a job for everyone, even Frank. Mama brought hot tea to warm us and I couldn't imagine a day being more special. But then winter came and Papa became sick with the influenza. From my bedroom window I'd look down at our winter beech, the leaves shimmying in the wind. One day Cooper cut some small beech limbs hanging with curled brown leaves. Midge and me put them in a jar and kept them on a table in our bedroom. I would look at the leaves and think for sure Papa would get better.

One Saturday I took the children out to rake up the leaves that were strewn over the verandah steps and in the front yard.

"I don't want an unsightly mess made," said Mrs. McMaster as we headed out the door.

"We never rake the leaves. That should be Firth and Trent's job," grumbled Sylvie.

"Well, today it's going to be our job," I said, picking up a leaf rake. "You never know how much fun something's going to be till you give it a try."

When Martha and Georgie picked up rakes, Sylvie scowled. "How can raking leaves be fun?" she said.

Martha stood beneath a maple tree and picked up a bright red leaf. "I think we should give it a try," she said.

"That's the spirit!"

"This isn't like Grandmother at all to let us come out here. We'll get dirty," Sylvie snapped, looking toward the house.

"I like the maple leaves," said Martha, blowing the leaf she was holding into the air.

"Me too," chimed Georgie. "Which one do you like, Lark?"

"The winter beech, of course, but there's none here in the dooryard. They're not a fancy colour like some of the others, but the winter beech has a secret."

"That's ridiculous! Trees can't have secrets," said Sylvie, kicking at a small pile of leaves on the ground by her feet.

"They most certainly can have secrets—at least the winter beech does." I smiled at Sylvie and she looked away. I'd hoped her attitude would change after the parcel incident.

"What's the secret?" Georgie demanded.

Martha and Georgie cried out for me to tell them the secret while Sylvie seemed not to care.

"The winter beech hangs on to its leaves all winter. They're brown and ordinary to look at, but special in their own way. It's like it's reminding us to never give up, even when common sense says we should."

"Everyone knows that trees lose their leaves in the fall," said Sylvie.

"Not the winter beech."

"But they do eventually fall off," said Sylvie, sounding annoyed once again.

"Only to make room for the new leaves that come in the spring."

"Sounds stupid to me," she said. "Just like raking leaves."

"Which reminds me—that's why we're here. Does everyone have a rake?" I handed Sylvie the one I was holding.

"Well, I'm not going to rake leaves and you can't make me," she said, throwing it to the ground. She stomped off and sat down on the verandah. Georgie ran through the leaves squealing and jumping, then flung himself on the ground.

"This can't be good for Georgie," said Sylvie distastefully from the verandah. "What if he gets dirty? Grandmother won't like it if you let him get dirty, Lark."

"Then we'll scrub him up squeaky clean so that he shines like a copper penny in the moonlight," I said. "Besides, I'm the one who washes the clothes. An extra pair of pants won't make a bit of difference to me."

"Sylvie's in a rotten mood because Rebecca O'Reily got a letter in the mail," said Martha. "No one sends us letters."

"Don't be dumb, Martha," said Sylvie. "What do I care if Rebecca gets mail or not?"

"Only the fact that she waved it under everybody's nose at school. It came from her aunt in the States," said Martha. She looked up at me. "Rebecca gets everything and it's not fair."

"Some things aren't fair, but complaining about it doesn't help one bit. So, let's rake these leaves before a wind comes along and blows them all the way into Rebecca O'Reily's backyard. Then she'll have all the fun of raking them."

We behaved like a troupe of clowns. Martha turned somersaults in the leaves while Georgie tried his best to imitate her. Sylvie sat on the steps like a bump on a log.

"Don't get dirty, Martha," she warned. "You're old enough to know better."

"What I know is that I'm having fun," called out Martha. "And if you were smart, you'd be having fun too, Sylvie."

"I'm warning you, Martha. Get up out of the leaves or I'll get you up."

Sylvie raced toward Martha. When she reached down to pull her up off the ground, Georgie charged at her. They both landed head over heels into the pile of leaves. Silence followed as we waited to see what Sylvie would do. I expected she would be madder than a wet cat, all claws and hisses. But just then Georgie pulled his head out from the pile of leaves, and what a comical sight he was. Leaves covered his head, A bright red one was stuck fast to his forehead. Sylvie looked over at him and started to giggle. Soon we were all laughing. Poor Georgie sat staring at Sylvie with his mouth stretched out as wide as a liquorice whip.

At last, we were finished. We had raked all the leaves into three huge piles.

"I like raking leaves," Sylvie admitted.

"You never know what fun you can have, Sylvie, till you try." I looked at her and smiled and this time her eyes softened. "I want to thank you all," I said, looking at them.

"For what?" asked Sylvie, looking confused.

"For helping me have fun. The last thing Mama said to me before I came here was, 'Make sure to have yourself some fun.' I almost forgot until now."

"I wish someone would tell Papa that," said Sylvie. We all looked at her in surprise.

"Papa used to have fun. Didn't he, Sylvie?" said Martha. "That's what you told me. You said he used to sing songs in the evening while Mama played the piano and he'd tell stories about when he was a small boy."

"Mama made him happy," said Sylvie. "Now all he has left is the three of us."

"And a lucky man he is to have three such wonderful children. Why, your father is rich by any man's standards."

For the very first time since I'd laid eyes on Mr. McMaster, I felt truly sorry for him. He was spending his days wishing for the past without appreciating what he had in the present.

"Now, let's hurry into the house before we get a talking to for staying out too long. Last one in's the rotten egg," I said, quickly changing the subject.

Little Georgie scurried toward the front door. "I'm winning! I'm winning!" he squealed, looking back at his sisters as he took the lead. We couldn't help laughing.

Reaching the verandah, I turned back toward the yard and smiled as I realized that I hadn't had this much fun since before Papa died. A lump formed in my throat, so hard I couldn't swallow. I wished I was back home. After Papa died, I couldn't imagine life going on without him, but it had. Guilt grabbed hold of me. Just as the leaves had turned to red and yellow, everything was changing without Papa there to see.

CHAPTER TWENTY-FOUR

ONE SATURDAY NEAR THE END OF NOVEMBER, MRS. MCMASTER CALLED the children into the kitchen. "I thought this year we'd make fruitcakes together," she announced, setting some empty bowls onto the table. She picked up a recipe book and opened it.

"You mean us?" Martha asked, looking toward her sister.

"Yes, of course," Mrs. McMaster replied sharply.

"But we don't know anything about baking," said Sylvie cautiously.

"Then you'll learn," Mrs. McMaster answered with impatience. She sighed. "For heaven's sake, I thought you'd be pleased." There was a hesitancy in her voice, as if she might be having a change of heart.

"It'll be great fun. I help Mama all the time," I said. "Just you wait and see."

I thought about all the times I helped Mama bake. Midge would sit perched onto a stool watching us measure things out.

Wonderful smells would fill the entire house on baking day. Papa would come into the kitchen and grab a warm cookie before Mama had time to scold him.

I looked around at the McMasters' big kitchen. What Mama's kitchen back home lacked in size, it more than made up for in the memories that had been made there. In that moment, I was struck with such longing for home that I didn't know what to do.

"There's an old family recipe I thought we'd use. It was one of your mother's favourites," said Mrs. McMaster. The children's faces lit up at the mention of their mother.

"Our mother?" asked Martha with curiosity.

"Certainly. Your mother was an excellent cook, always perfecting her recipes; an extra pinch here, a dash there. There are some who would have done just about anything to have her recipe for dark fruitcake."

The children looked at one another, grinning. They suddenly appeared glad to be helping.

We gathered the ingredients for the fruitcakes while Mrs. McMaster searched through her recipe book. I measured out the flour while Mrs. McMaster added the molasses. Sylvie helped break open eggs while Martha added the spices and raisins.

"I suspect you've helped make fruitcakes before, Lark," said Mrs. McMaster, measuring out some flour.

I nodded, wishing I was back in Mama's kitchen making new memories. I wouldn't even care if Midge and Frank were in the way, reaching into the bowl and sucking cake batter from their fingers.

"You've been rather quiet lately," Mrs. McMaster said, handing me the cake pan.

I swallowed, hard. "I've been missing my family something wicked—this past while especially," I said, spreading the pan with grease.

"I was beginning to wonder if you hadn't run out of words, the way you sometimes rattle on," she said, lining the cake pan with brown paper. "Well, at least you haven't some incurable disease. You'll snap out of it soon enough. So long as it doesn't interfere with your work."

"It won't, Mrs. McMaster," I said as bravely as I could.

"I must say, I'm glad to hear that…Have you added the salt, Sylvie?" she asked, turning her attention back to the girls.

Mrs. McMaster towered over the bowls. Every now and again she'd dip a spoon into the batter and take a taste to make sure there were enough spices.

Georgie sat on a stool by the table waiting for a spoon or empty bowl to be passed his way. "Can I have a lick?" he'd ask every so often.

When Sylvie finally handed him a spoon you'd have thought he had a million pennies.

"Put your tongue to that, Georgie," she said, "and never mind the toothache you're bound to get."

He grabbed the spoon from his sister's hand and scrambled off into a corner to lick it clean. We all laughed.

"That's right," Mrs. McMaster said, looking amused. "Crawl in the corner, George. You never know who'll take that spoon from you."

We laughed even harder. But that didn't bother little George. He sat in the corner with his mouth stretched open like a pumpkin grinner's. I was sure he was never going to stop.

Once the cakes were baked and cooled, Mrs. McMaster sealed them away in tin cans to ripen and then hid them in some remote part of the pantry, and no one but she knew the location. This added to the mystery and excitement of the upcoming holiday.

In preparation for Christmas, Mrs. McMaster insisted that everything must be cleaned. The walls in the parlour and kitchen were washed, the floors scoured and waxed.

"You're doing a fine job, Lark," she said when I had the last floor waxed.

For once I didn't say a thing. I was so homesick I didn't quite know what to do with myself. The lump in my throat had grown. It wouldn't go up and it wouldn't go down.

I confided as much to Brock Cameron one day while mixing a batch of biscuits.

"It's a miserable feeling," said Brock, spreading a hearty slice of bread. "And it don't matter how old you are. I've known grown folks who get sick to the heart when they were away from home. I remember the first time I got homesick. Couldn't eat or sleep. It'll pass, though. Always does, given enough time."

"Have you seen Mama and the others lately?" I asked, hoping for even a smidgeon of news he might be carrying from home.

"Just the other day, as a matter of fact. Your mother was asking all about you," said Brock, giving me a wink, and then he recounted everything Mama had said.

His words brought me comfort. I devoured them like a ravenous whiskey jack in the dead of winter. His stories were like fairy tales, fables of long ago and far away, where Cooper and Frank were both handsome princes and Midge the beautiful princess who captured the hearts of those far and wide. Mama was the regal queen who ruled with wisdom and patience over them all. In a strange way it felt as though Brock had caught them up in a big lasso and pulled them right into the kitchen beside me. I could feel them in my heart, laughing and talking, their voices sounding like a sweet melody in my ear. How I wished I could see them for even a short time.

Chapter Twenty-Five

ALTHOUGH MRS. MCMASTER NEVER SAID, I'M SURE BROCK HAD SOMEthing to do with her allowing me to go home for a short visit that fall.

"Pack your bag, Lark Harnish," she said one Friday morning in early December. "I believe a few days at home are in order. You may go with Brock Cameron today, but I expect you to be back come Tuesday morning with the mail."

Holding back my joy was next to impossible. I grabbed onto Mrs. McMaster and gave her a big squeeze. "You won't regret this, Mrs. McMaster, not one little bit. I'll come back a new person, you'll see." I danced a few steps right there in the kitchen. This was the best surprise I could have imagined.

"Oh for goodness' sake, Lark Harnish, must you carry on so?"

"I can't help it, Mrs. McMaster. Haven't you ever wanted to cut loose and shout from the rooftops?"

"And have Bertha Gray think I've gone senile? I hardly think so."

However, my joy was short-lived, as Mr. McMaster walked into the kitchen at just that moment.

"What is the meaning of this?" he asked, shooting his mother a questioning look. He seated himself at the table. Mrs. McMaster set a plate of hot biscuits down and he reached for one. I set a plate of fried baked beans and sausages in front of him and went to fix plates for Firth and Trent.

"I was simply telling Lark that she might have a few days off to go home. She's been working hard. I thought she deserved a reward."

"Going home!" said Trent coming through the porch door. "I'd say it's about time." He and Firth took their place at the table. I set their breakfast in front of them, about to burst into a ripple of happiness.

"Just a moment here," said Mr. McMaster, clearing his throat. "Are you sure we can spare Lark for that long? The work will only pile up. Too late once she's gone." He gave his mother a serious look.

"For land's sakes, we managed long before Lark Harnish ever graced us with her presence," said Mrs. McMaster, pouring tea for the men. "I'm hardly an invalid."

"You're not used to carrying the entire burden now, and then there's the post office," added Mr. McMaster, reaching for his fork. "Lark's place is here, helping you."

My heart screamed at the injustice of it all. It had been months since I'd seen my family, and just you wait, Mr. McMaster was going to ruin it all for me. The thought infuriated me to the core. For him to try and take that away from me was a downright cold-hearted thing, even for Mr. McMaster. He was just trying to be difficult. Anger boiled inside me like a red-hot teakettle.

If I didn't speak up, I would explode into a cloud of steam right there in front of him.

"Why, you old meanie," I said, "this is between your mother and me." All eyes veered my way. "You just can't stand to see anyone the least bit happy, can you? You walk around with your face dragging in the dirt and you can't even muster up a grin if your life depended upon in. Not even for your own children, you can't. I'm sorry your wife died." Mrs. McMaster gasped. A table knife clattered onto the floor just as Sylvie and Martha walked in. They stopped abruptly. "I'm sorry because it's turned you cold and miserable. But I won't have you ruining this for me. I'm going home. That's just the way it is, and if come Tuesday there's no job for me here, then that's the way it'll have to be."

I didn't wait for his reaction. I stomped off through the kitchen, my cheeks a burning red ember. Martha looked as though she was about to say something until Sylvie quieted her with a tap on the arm.

"We'll see about that, Lark Harnish!" Mr. McMaster said coldly. "We'll just see about that."

I hastily folded my belongings and placed them in my bag. Never in my days had I known anyone as disagreeable as Mr. McMaster. He angered me so, I could scarcely think properly. All this time he'd been cold and distant, as if a few words of praise to me would kill him right there on the spot. Not one speck of encouragement, not even when I proved I could work alongside the men when I was needed. I'd even saved the farm from the fire. What more did he want from me?

"Well, you won't stop me, Mr. McMaster," I said, looking at my refection in the mirror. "You might be the king around here, but you don't rule over me. No sir, George Stanley McMaster. I'm not Sylvie or Martha, or little George. I'm not even your mother.

I'm not trapped here in your mighty castle...You can't keep me against my will!"

Tears of frustration blurred my eyes. How would Mama ever make ends meet if I lost my job with the McMasters now? I should have kept my mouth shut. But how could I? Not when my hopes of seeing everyone back home had been raised to such a high degree that my head was laughing with the sheer excitement of it all. Oh, why did Mr. McMaster have to be such an ogre?

With my fingers clasped around my bag, I was ready to dash down the stairs the moment I heard the tinkle of Brock Cameron's horse bells. But before that could happen, a tap came to my bedroom door and it squeaked open. Mrs. McMaster stood quietly in front of me. I looked at her sheepishly, ashamed of my earlier outburst. I had behaved like a child, there was no denying it. She looked at my packed bag, clutched tightly in my hands.

"I don't approve of the tone you used with George Stanley at all. While you do work for me, he's the one who pays you each week." She started out slowly, her voice quiet and flat. I didn't answer. I'd spoken out when I shouldn't have. A hired girl should know her place, and that place most certainly wasn't talking back to the very person who was paying her wages. I had acted in a most ungrateful way and allowed my bitter disappointment to rule my head. I deserved whatever came next.

"I'm willing to overlook the things you said, seeing the state you've been in this past while," Mrs. McMaster continued. "You must know that George Stanley would never suggest you aren't entitled to go home for a visit. You're a hard worker. You've already proven yourself. He can see that. His concern, naturally, is for me. He worries that there's too much work for me at my age. George Stanley is a fair man, but like his father before him, he expects a great deal from the people he employs. Perhaps sometimes a bit too much." She moved toward the window and pulled back the curtain.

"Now, I've spoken with George Stanley and he agrees you deserve to have some time off. I suppose when all is said and done, it was my fault for not having discussed this with him beforehand. George Stanley does not like surprises."

Mrs. McMaster was not the only one who let out a deep breath once she'd finished. I was as relieved as she sounded.

"Now bring your bag along. Brock Cameron will be here shortly," said Mrs. McMaster. And as she turned back toward the door, there was no mistaking the look of pleasure that meandered across her face.

Chapter Twenty-Six

HOW WONDERFUL IT FELT TO BE BACK IN CRAWFORDVILLE. Mama was as surprised as anyone when I walked into the kitchen unannounced. I dropped my bag and threw my arms around her. As I looked about the kitchen, our house felt suddenly small, but I would gladly take a house filled with love over a spacious one filled only with grief and longing.

"Something smells good," I said, smiling as I looked all around the kitchen. I detected the spicy aroma of fresh-baked gingerbread and Mama's homemade bread. My heart swelled with happiness as all the little things I loved about home came rushing back to me.

"It's so good to have you home," Mama said after supper. She studied me for the longest while. "Why, you've grown so tall. Hasn't she grown tall?" she asked, looking from Cooper to Midge and Frank.

"I haven't been gone *that* long," I laughed.

"It seems like forever," piped up Frank. "Your hair grew." We laughed ourselves silly until he finally asked what he'd said that was so funny. But we weren't laughing about what Frank had said; we were laughing out of happiness and nothing more.

Later, Frank pulled off the worst shenanigans, jumping up and down and waving his arms in the air.

"Look at me, Lark!" he'd squeal while trying to stand on his head or turn a somersault. If no one paid him any mind he'd stick his face in front of ours and ask, "Can you see me? Can you see me?"

"Frank," I said finally, "we'd all have to be blindfolded not to see you." Everyone laughed, including Frank, who didn't stop to think that his constant badgering might be annoying.

"You've changed, Lark," Mama said that evening as we washed the supper dishes.

"Why, of course I've changed. And so have you and Frank and Cooper and Midge. Everyone changes. That's what life is all about."

"There was a time when I thought change was bad," said Mama, wiping a dinner plate.

"Sometimes it's not very nice," I said, thinking of how Papa was gone from us. I could tell Mama was thinking the same. We worked in silence for a spell, savouring our own private thoughts.

"Brock Cameron says I've brought a lot of changes to the McMasters' household," I said once the dishes were done.

Mama smiled and folded the cup towel. "I'm sure they had no idea what they were getting themselves into when you arrived."

I laughed. "Indeed, I believe you're right."

"Tell us some stories, Lark," Frank begged as we gathered in the parlour later that evening. I looked around at the eager faces before me. I had a mountain of stories to tell but scarcely knew where to begin. Taking some time to collect my thoughts, I started at the beginning, at the first day I arrived. I told them all about the horses and cattle and the day I helped with the hay. I told them about the children and how sad it was that their mother had died and how everyone in the house missed her. I even told them about the how busy the house is when the mail arrives and the day me and Mrs. McMaster put out the fire.

At bedtime Midge and I climbed up into the loft. I curled around her the way I used to on cold winter nights when the wind whistled in around the windowpanes.

"It's strange without you here," whispered Midge in the quiet of our room. The sound of her voice told me she had her thumb stuck in her mouth.

"It's strange without you there." I reached across and pulled her thumb out of her mouth.

"Do you think you'll come home to live again forever and ever?" said Midge, sitting up in the dark.

"I'm not really sure. Mama needs my help."

"Cooper helps out."

"I guess I'm doing it for everyone, then." I was afraid if I said too much, I might start to feel sorry for myself, and a sorry heart never accomplished a thing. At least that's what I overheard Mrs. McMaster say to her son one day when she thought no one could hear.

"What about Mrs. McMaster? Are you doing it for her, too?" Midge settled back down in bed and I tucked the quilt about her neck.

"Yes, for Mrs. McMaster."

"And the children?"

"Yes, the children."

"And the horses and pig and the cows?" Sleepy sounds were gathering in her voice.

"Yes, all those things...Now go to sleep."

"Go to sleep, Lark," she yawned. But I couldn't sleep. I was home for a few days and I didn't want to miss a single moment of time. My mind spun thinking of all the things I would do come morning, all the places I would visit. For the first time in nearly four months, I didn't have to worry that Mrs. McMaster would scold me for not paying attention to what I was doing.

CHAPTER TWENTY-SEVEN

THE NEXT MORNING, WE WENT TO THE BARN TO SEARCH FOR FLUFFY. She came running the minute Frank rattled her dish. She curled around my legs and purred.

"I missed you, Fluffy," I said, picking her up. More interested in what Frank had put in her dish than being held, Fluffy jumped out of my arms and went to investigate the scraps. A small orange ball of fur stepped out from behind a bale of straw and made its way to the feeding dish.

"Where are the rest of her babies?" I asked.

"Cooper gave one to Mr. Nichols at the blacksmith shop and Mrs. Hobbs took the other. Mrs. Hobbs said it would be good company for her since she lost that tabby cat of hers last year. We're keeping the orange one," Midge added.

Frank picked him up and he squirmed to get away.

"He's hungry, too," I said stroking his fur.

"I wanted to call him Orangie, but Midge and Cooper said that's a stupid name," said Frank.

"How about Marmalade, then? Marmalade's made of oranges." Frank and Midge looked at one another and nodded. "Well then, Marmalade it is."

Midge and Frank could scarcely wait to tell Mama the new name for the kitten. Mama laughed. "I've been trying to get those two to agree on a name for the longest while," she said. "And just like that you settled it, Lark."

After dinner, I went to say hello to Mrs. Hobbs. "Please come in, dear Lark," she said. "I've something to show you."

Mrs. Hobbs welcomed me into her parlour. "Look up there," she said. Stretched across the mantel beside her porcelain doll was the black kitten. "I call her Midnight, and, oh dear me, the joy she's brought to this house. It's her favourite place to sleep."

"I'm surprised she hasn't knocked everything off the mantel. It would be a shame for your doll," I said.

"Oh no, not my Midnight," she said, lifting the kitten gently into her arms. Purring loudly, the kitten crawled up around Mrs. Hobbs' neck. I brushed Midnight's shiny coat. "You wouldn't knock over Diana would you, Midnight?"

The kitten meowed in reply.

"It's as if she understands everything I say." Mrs. Hobbs smiled with more pride than a mother cat.

I told Mrs. Hobbs that I'd been putting the stationery she gave me to good use.

"Oh yes, my dear. I've been following along with your adventures. Your mother reads your letters to me. And what adventures you've been having," she said. Midnight's long tail curled about her face.

Although I would have liked to have stayed longer, I said my goodbyes to Mrs. Hobbs and Midnight.

"You're a good girl, Lark Harnish, to be helping out your mother the way you are. Everyone here in Crawfordville is proud of you for what you're doing," Mrs. Hobbs called out to me as I left.

I walked all about the village, past Mr. Hubley's store and the sawmill. I could hear Mr. Nichols in his blacksmith shop hitting his anvil, and I wondered what Cooper might be doing on a Saturday afternoon inside the shop.

"Most times I just keep the forge going," Cooper had told me last night, "and sweep up around. If I'm lucky I get to swing the hammer. I'm learning to make horseshoes now."

"I do my share of sweeping too," I said and we laughed.

On Sunday morning, some songbirds followed us on our way to church. Midge and Frank hurried on ahead. They were each carrying a nickel for the collection plate and feeling quite proud about it. They kept peeking between their fingers to make sure it was still there. Mama called out to them several times, "Don't lose your offering or you'll answer to Reverend Bradley."

As Midge scurried past Frank, I cried out that we'd do something special after church if she behaved and listened to Mama. Not wanting to miss out on a fun opportunity, whatever that would be, she slowed down and walked the rest of the way.

I'm sure Mama was relieved when Cliff Peterson took up the collection and Midge's and Frank's nickels tinkled against the bottom of the plate. When the pump organ started up, the entire congregation began to sing. The music that rang out from the church sounded as if it was coming from heaven.

Once the service was over, Mama stood outside talking to the neighbours. They wanted to know how I was doing and what it was like working for the McMaster family. I hadn't been to church since I left Crawfordville in late August. The McMasters faithfully attended church in Upper Springdale, but I was never invited to go along.

"How would you like to receive a letter?" I asked Midge once we got home from church. I hadn't forgotten the promise I'd made her earlier that morning. I'd been thinking for some time how much Sylvie and Martha would enjoy receiving a letter, and I knew Midge would too.

"I love getting letters," squealed Midge.

"Well, I know two girls who would love to get a letter just as much as you. Only, neither one of them ever got one before."

Midge looked at me with a gleam in her eyes. "You mean Sylvie and Martha, don't you?"

"None other. You should have a great lot in common. Sylvie's nearly eleven and Martha's nine. It tears them up, all those letters coming to the house and never one for them. Maybe you could become writing pals."

"But what would I write about? And would we send it through the mail?"

"Write about yourself. Tell them the things you like to do. What makes you happy and what you like best about living in Crawfordville. They might like to hear about Marmalade's escapades. It won't be difficult. And of course it must be official, sent through the post office. It just wouldn't be the same if I handed it to them."

How well I understood that magical feeling when a letter arrived stamped and postmarked. I knew Sylvie and Martha would feel the same. With a bit of guidance from me, Midge wrote the most delightful message. She even drew a picture of herself.

"Do you think they'll be excited?" she asked, licking the envelope and sealing it shut.

"I know for a fact they will." I could hardly wait to see the looks on their faces when the letter arrived.

Excitement swelled inside me as we started up the McMasters' long drive on Tuesday morning. How different it felt from the first time I drove up with Brock and Bella. Being home made me realize just how important my job was to our family. Mama was slowly getting the grocery bill paid off and in time she'd be completely out of debt.

Little George ran out to greet me.

"You're back, Lark!" said Georgie, jumping up and down.

"Of course I'm back. They'd have to tie me up and gag me to keep me away."

Mrs. McMaster stood in the doorway, watching as Brock helped me down from his buggy. "Pity the poor fool who'd try and gag you," she said, her arms folded in front of her. "I trust your visit was a prosperous one?"

"Indeed, Mrs. McMaster, very prosperous." I knew that was her way of asking if my homesickness was gone.

"Very good. There's an ocean of work to be done. Come along," she said. And if I wasn't sure, I'd almost be inclined to think she looked the slightest bit pleased to see me.

CHAPTER TWENTY-EIGHT

THE POST OFFICE WAS LIKE A BEEHIVE THOSE LAST WEEKS BEFORE Christmas, with people sending off cards and parcels. As busy as what she was, I'd never seen Mrs. McMaster look so content.

"She looks quite happy," said Sylvie, peering into the post office from a safe distance. The post office was closed up for the day, but when Mrs. Fraser walked in toting some sizeable parcels, Mrs. McMaster didn't have the heart to send her away.

"Now, these won't go until next Tuesday," she said, speaking loud enough for Mrs. Fraser to hear.

"Yes, dear, it's good of you to fix it up for me," she said, patting Mrs. McMaster's hand.

"It must be the glue on the stamps," Martha said, watching her grandmother put the postage on Mrs. Fraser's parcel. "Perhaps the glue tastes good. It seems to make Grandmother happy."

"Maybe it's the holiday season," I said. "Everyone appears to be in a good mood. It's all the good will toward men, like in the Christmas carol."

"And grandmothers," piped in Martha.

The day Sylvie and Martha received their letter from Midge, you'd have thought it had been sent by the queen. They danced in a circle with their hands joined together.

"I've never seen a little bit of mail cause such a commotion," said Mrs. McMaster. I laughed to see their excitement.

"You knew, Lark, didn't you?" said Sylvie.

"Indeed, I could scarcely keep it to myself these past days."

"Wait until Rebecca sees this. Her letter was from her aunt. Her mother probably begged her to write it." Martha laughed, dancing about with the letter in her hand. "This one came all on its own."

"I'll bet she doesn't say a word," said Sylvie, snatching it from Martha's fingers.

"I'll bet you're right," agreed Martha, grabbing it back. And off they went to read the letter again.

Martha and Sylvie were not the only ones to get a surprise in the mail that day. Mama sent me a card that Midge had made. It said, *May Your Christmas Be Merry*, only she had spelled *Merry* as *Mary* and had crossed it out and spelled it correctly. It made me smile. On the front was a Christmas tree far too small for the presents she had drawn. On the inside were four people and she'd written the names beneath the pictures. Mama, Frank, Cooper, Midge. Beneath their faces she wrote, *We miss you, Lark.*

A long string of Christmas cards hung from one corner of the parlour to the other. The McMasters had many family and friends. Each mail day brought with it more cards.

"I know it's early to be stringing up the cards, but I thought it might help to put everyone in the Christmas spirit. One year we got eighty-three cards." I wondered who all she meant when she said "everyone." Did I detect a pinch of excitement in her voice as she strung up the cards that had arrived in the mail that day? I finally decided I must be mistaken, because I was almost certain there was nothing in this world that ever made Mrs. McMaster excited. Not even Christmas.

"They're all so beautiful," I agreed. "It's too bad we couldn't leave them up all year."

"This one's my favourite," said Mrs. McMaster, pointing to a brightly decorated card with a nativity scene. "The best part about Christmas is the cards. It lets you know who's thinking of you."

$$\infty$$

One evening a knock came at my bedroom door. I could hear Martha and Georgie on the other side gibbering back and forth. I swung the door open and feigned surprise upon seeing them.

"Can we come in?" asked Martha in a shy voice.

"You're always welcome to visit," I said. They climbed up onto my bed.

"We'd like a story, Lark," Georgie stated quite seriously.

"Something Christmassy," said Martha, her eyes shining. "Sylvie says our mother used to tell stories, and I think it would be quite nice to hear one. Grandmother says she doesn't know any and it's a waste of her time trying to concoct one. She says her imagination is as dull as a butter knife."

"Well now, you've hardly given me enough notice. Suppose my story ends up putting you to sleep?"

"No one ever told me a Christmas story before, not that I can remember," said Georgie.

I sat down on the bed next to them. I had tons of stories, but which one should I choose? I thought for a few moments. "Now, you mustn't make fun," I told them. "I'm not a writer or a storyteller by nature, but Mama does say I have the gift of gab, so we'll see." Another knock came at the door and it opened slowly.

"Can I come in too?" asked Sylvie meekly.

"Only if you want to hear a story," I told her. She smiled and hurried toward my bed. The glow from the oil lamp illuminated their faces as they sat waiting for me to start.

"Lark's going to tell us a Christmas story," said Georgie, his eyes sparkling like flecks of ice. Sylvie climbed up on the bed beside me.

"Have you ever gone belsnickeling?" I asked, adding the sound of mystery to my voice.

"Papa says we're too young," said Sylvie.

"Well, I remember one Christmas when my father said much the same thing to me. And it hardly seemed fair considering he was taking my older brother, Cooper."

"What did you do, Lark?" Martha looked at me with disbelieving eyes.

"I went off on my own, of course. No one was going to get ahead of me. Made myself a Santa Claus suit without anyone knowing. I even sewed rabbit fur around the collar to make it official."

"Real fur!" squealed Georgie, bouncing up and down on the bed.

"Papa and Cooper were tending rabbit snares that year and were having good luck catching them. I used some of the fur. They never guessed."

"What did you do then?" asked Georgie.

"Would you stop asking so many questions, and let Lark tell the story?" growled Sylvie. I put my finger to my lips, motioning for everyone to be quiet.

"What did I do next? Why, I made myself a mask out of flour paste and brown paper so no one would know who I was. That night, once the barn chores were done, Papa told Cooper to get geared up to go belsnickeling. I waited for them to leave, then told Mama I was going to the barn to groom the horses. This was back when Papa had four horses in the barn. A beautiful chestnut mare, his team of Clydesdales that he used to take to horse pulls all over the countryside, and of course, Jim. Papa was a good horse trader. I liked to spend time in the barn slicking up the horses' hair and making them shiny, so Mama never thought a thing about it when I said I was going out into the barn that night.

"'Make sure you take a lantern' was all she said. She even lit it for me. Of course, when I got to the barn I had my costume hidden behind the tub of short feed. I got myself rigged up and off I went."

"Didn't you get caught, Lark?" asked Georgie, unable to resist the temptation to ask another question. He looked toward Sylvie to see if he would get another scolding.

"Get caught? I should think not! Every place I went they stared at me like I was from the moon. Some tried to trick me and get me to say something. 'Would you like another cookie, or how about some sweet cider? Take your mask off and eat your treat before you leave.' Well, I wasn't about to do that! They'd figure out who I was, and that's the whole idea, to stump everyone and make them wonder. It was a beautiful night for walking. On my way from Clive Jenkins's house I recognized the sound of the bells on Papa's sleigh coming from up the road. They were on their way home."

"Did you get caught then, Lark?" asked Georgie again.

"Me? Get caught? Not likely. I hid near the side of the road where I wouldn't be seen and waited for Papa's sleigh to go past. When Jim trotted by, I listened for the shush of the runners before hurrying to the side of the road. And when Papa and Cooper drove by, I jumped onto the runners and held fast to the sleigh. And my, what a ride I had! Twice I nearly lost my grip, but I managed to hang on until I saw the light from our kitchen window.

"I jumped off when the sleigh got to the end of our driveway. I crept up the driveway in the dark while Papa and Cooper unhooked Jim and took him into the barn. While they unharnessed Jim, I went for my lantern where I'd hidden it outside in the shadows. They never suspected a thing. I slipped into the house without Mama finding out. I balled my costume up and hid it in the trunk in my bedroom. And do you know, I don't think anyone to this day has ever figured out who that mysterious belsnickeler was."

I looked around at the smiling faces before me. They all agreed it was one of the best Christmas stories they'd ever heard.

"I wish I had a Christmas story to tell," said George, climbing down from the bed.

"We all have stories, Georgie," I said. "Sooner or later, you will too."

"Do you think so, Lark?" he asked with a gleam in his eye.

"I'm positive."

The children left my room more excited than ever for Christmas morning to come. Soon I heard a quiet tapping on my door. It was Sylvie.

"I'm sorry," she said, her head drooping.

"Sorry?" I wasn't sure what she meant.

"About reading your letter. You seemed so happy, I wanted to know what your family was like. I saw it in your room and the envelope wasn't sealed."

"Apology accepted," I said with a smile. I hadn't imagined Sylvie would ever apologize, but there was genuine regret in her voice. "Just one thing," I said as she went to leave. She turned toward me. "Can we be friends, now?"

Sylvie smiled. "Yes, please," she said. "I'd like that."

CHAPTER TWENTY-NINE

MR. MCMASTER WENT OUT TO CUT THE TREE TWO DAYS BEFORE Christmas, but only because Martha and Sylvie pestered him relentlessly until he gave in.

"I don't like to put a tree up too early. Used to be you didn't put up a tree till Christmas Eve," he grumbled as he went for his boots.

"Can I come with you, Papa?" asked little George, watching his father put on his coat and hat. "I can help pick out a good tree."

"You're too little. Besides, you can't walk that far in the snow. You'll end up lying in a snowbank too tired to move. I can't drag you *and* a tree home."

Georgie sat by the window watching his father cross the snowy, windswept field. He was wearing a frown so furrowed I thought he might trip over his bottom lip if he moved from his chair.

"Cheer up, Georgie," I told him sunnily. "Santa will soon be coming and he won't want to see a glum boy."

"You don't want a lump of coal, do you, Georgie?" asked Martha.

"Coal is for bad boys, not glum boys," corrected Sylvie.

Soon Georgie was squealing, jumping up and down with excitement. "Here comes Papa with our tree!"

Across the pasture came Mr. McMaster dragging a bushy tree behind him.

"It's the biggest tree yet," laughed Martha, clapping her hands wildly as she watched from the window.

Indeed, it was the grandest tree I'd ever seen. Its branches spread wide. Our parlour was much smaller than the one in the McMaster home. We'd never have room for a tree that size.

Mr. McMaster set the tree inside the porch to dry off.

"I can help!" cried Georgie, dashing toward it. He grabbed fast to one of the branches and began to pull.

"Stay back. You're just in the way. You'll break the branches and there'll be nothing to hang the ornaments on," growled his father. Little George groaned and stepped aside. Everyone was so busy looking through the box of decorations they hadn't even noticed that Mr. McMaster had scolded little George. Brock Cameron had said the household was changing, but that change didn't seem to include Mr. McMaster, who was the same grumpy man I'd met four months ago.

Mama used to tell Papa he was the biggest kid of all when it came to Christmas. He didn't want to miss a single moment. He'd take us all out to cut a tree and then he'd help Mama get the Christmas box down from the loft. And never a tree decorating took place in our house without singing Christmas carols.

Later that day, Mr. McMaster dragged the tree into the parlour and wrestled it into the stand. Had he not been so insistent about not needing help, it wouldn't have taken half the time.

"There, I've done my part," he said, crawling out from beneath the tree. "The rest is up to all of you."

"You can help if you'd like," I suggested. I'd probably regret saying it, but it was Christmastime, and miracles have been said to happen around the holidays. I figured the children would like their father to help. Mr. McMaster looked as though he were about to bark at me for suggesting such a thing, until Mrs. McMaster spoke up.

"It's been a long time, George Stanley. Don't you remember how Dorothy loved decorating the tree? She used to sing."

When the children heard this, they begged their father to join in, but the mean old grouch left the parlour without hanging a single ornament.

"Who wants to decorate?" I said. The children yelled out that they did. I wasn't about to let him stop us from enjoying the day.

Georgie and I were put in charge of making the popcorn and Mrs. McMaster helped the girls string it.

"This was always Dorothy's job," said Mrs. McMaster, reaching into the bowl of popped corn. The children looked at her with curiosity. "Oh, I'm sorry," she said when she realized she was being stared at. "Christmas makes me sentimental. Silly, isn't it?"

"It's not silly at all. I'm sure the children would love to hear stories about their mother. Wouldn't you?" I said, smiling at the three yearning faces before me.

"Oh, I'm hardly a storyteller. I don't have a knack for detail… or description for that matter." Mrs. McMaster looked over at me and smiled. "I don't have a flare for relating yarns the way you do, Lark Harnish."

"Please, Grandmother," Sylvie pleaded. "There are so many things I don't remember. And Martha and George just want to know anything."

"I'm sure you remember something," I coaxed. "If you share your memories, the children will get to know their mother a little better."

Mrs. McMaster hesitated, then went to the box of decorations. She took out one of the ornaments and carefully unwrapped the newspaper. Inside was a round silver ball.

"Your mother made these ornaments," she said, holding it up by the thin string. "She saved up the lead from tea packages because she wanted silver balls for on her tree. She even enlisted the help from some of the neighbours. Oh my, the tea lead she had that one year. I wondered at the time what she would do with it all. Jimmy Hebb's mother, God rest her soul, swore she drank more tea than the Queen of England just to help Dorothy out. And your mother was always doing for others. She'd make these little cakes and set them on doorsteps at Christmastime to surprise the old people. Not to take credit, mind you. She kept those good deeds a secret."

Reaching into the box again, this time Mrs. McMaster removed some crepe-paper chains. "She made these as well."

The children moved closer so they might see the ornaments better.

"Some people would save the popcorn from year to year, but not Dorothy. She'd take it out and hang it in the trees for the birds once the tree was taken down. She said even the birds deserved to have a Christmas…She was always thinking of someone."

Mrs. McMaster gave a small sigh. Reaching back inside the box, she removed a star.

"With the rest of the tea lead she made this star for the tree-top. Dorothy said you couldn't have a Christmas tree without the star of Bethlehem smiling down over us all. She liked to make things with her hands. She had that certain touch. And your father took such delight in the things she made. He used to say that one day he'd open a store so she could sell all the things she made. She…" A faraway look spread across Mrs. McMaster's face. She stopped talking, set the box down, and moved toward the window. She stared out at the snowy pasture.

Reaching into the bottom of the box, little George pulled out a tiny silver ornament. "It doesn't have a string," he said. Mrs. McMaster took it from him and gasped.

"It was the last one Dorothy was working on when she ran out of lead. She was planning to save more, for the next year, but then…" She stopped speaking.

"Can I have it?" asked little George.

"Have it? Whatever for? It can't even be hung on the tree. It needs more lead."

"It'll remind me of Mama," said little George. "Like the winter beech leaves remind you of your father, right Lark?" He looked at me, smiling.

Just then, Mr. McMaster came back into the parlour. "Put that away," he said when he saw Georgie holding the ornament.

"George Stanley…don't," spoke up Mrs. McMaster when he grabbed the ornament.

He stopped and glared at his mother. "It's not finished," he barked.

"It would mean a lot to little George. It was the last one Dorothy was working on." A pained look crossed Mr. McMaster's face as he lay the ornament down and marched out of the room.

I felt sorry for Georgie—for them all. Mama says the memories you have of someone keeps them alive in your heart. By keeping his memories bottled up inside, Mr. McMaster was robbing the children of ever knowing their mother.

Sylvie and Martha and Georgie waited for Mrs. McMaster to say something more. She turned back toward them. There was a small tear in the corner of her left eye.

"Do you have enough popcorn?" she asked. "If we don't hurry up, Christmas will be here and gone before this tree ever gets decorated."

Chapter Thirty

O N CHRISTMAS EVE, MOTHER NATURE COVERED EVERYTHING WITH A thick blanket of frosty snow. Sylvie and Martha were worried that Santa wouldn't find them because of it. Their fears were put to rest the moment they came downstairs the next morning.

After breakfast, we gathered around the Christmas tree to open presents. Everyone was dressed up in their finest clothes. It was Christmas Day, a time to be merry and give thanks for all the good things that had happened during the year. I thought about my time here in Upper Springdale and all the experiences I'd had. Mrs. McMaster had said I could go home for a few days. She'd talked it over with Mr. McMaster and he'd agreed. Brock Cameron would be back for the mail in three days and I was more excited than any one person could be.

"Can I help light the candles?" little George asked now.

Begrudgingly, Mr. McMaster nodded his head. "Don't spill any wax on your grandmother's floor," he said, steadying the match in Georgie's hand. "Fire is a dangerous thing. You have to be careful."

Mrs. McMaster sighed. "Must you take the fun out of everything? He's just a boy."

Ignoring her remark, he continued to help Georgie with the candles. Santa brought each one of the girls a porcelain doll with a pink-and-white dress. They looked like twins in their matching get-ups, even their father said so. Little George got the brand-spanking-new sled he'd been hinting about for months. He was as pleased as any boy could be and immediately wanted to take it outside for a run.

"Maybe later," said Mr. McMaster. "You haven't had your orange yet. Your ribbon candy, either."

"Please, Papa," begged little George. "I want to try out my sled."

"I have to do the barn chores," Mr. McMaster said. "Horses and cows don't wait for Christmas celebrations. They still need to eat."

"After you feed the horses, then?" asked little George.

"We'll see," Mr. McMaster mumbled. "It's awfully windy out." Little George's pleading tugged at my heart. He looked like a boy who'd gotten the lump of coal for Christmas instead of a fancy new sled.

"Come, Georgie," said Sylvie. "You can show me your sled once the gifts are all opened." Little George reluctantly agreed. Sylvie took his hand and lead him over to the settee. I only wished there was something I could do. I'd have offered to take him outside but Mrs. McMaster would need my help in the kitchen all day.

When the last of the gifts were unwrapped, there remained a parcel wrapped in brown paper beneath the tree.

"It arrived last week," said Mrs. McMaster, handing it to me. "And the job I had to keep you from seeing it."

I untied the string, resisting the urge to tear it apart. Inside were knitted socks and mitts. I held them close and breathed in the scent of home. Instantly, I could see them—Mama, Midge, Frank, and Cooper—standing by the Christmas tree. I breathed again. Frank and Midge were running toward the windowsill, craning to see what Santa had put in their shoes. Another deep breath and Cooper was lighting the candles on the tree. I could smell the chestnuts roasting in the kitchen oven, and there was Mama all prettied up for the day. I saw, and smelled, it all.

Mrs. McMaster presented me with an orange and a small bag of ribbon candy.

"I never had an orange before!" I gasped, rolling it in my hands before taking a sniff. It smelled like nothing I could have ever imagined. My mouth watered and my nose tingled. And when I laughed out loud, Mrs. McMaster managed a smile.

"If you're not planning to eat it right away, put it in your dresser drawer. The smell will linger in your clothes for weeks," she said.

"I bet Trent would take me sledding if he was here. I wish he hadn't gone home for Christmas," said little George.

"George!" scolded Mrs. McMaster. "It's Christmas Day, and I should hope you would be happy that Trent and Firth were lucky enough to find a way home to be with their family."

"Sorry," he said, his head hanging low.

Mrs. McMaster jumped to her feet. "Let's not dwell on this. Not on Christmas Day," she said, clapping her hands together. "You'll have a chance to try out your sled. Just be patient." I knew that telling a five-year-old to be patient was like setting a horse loose in a field and expecting it not to run off.

I helped Mrs. McMaster prepare the meal. We peeled carrots and potatoes and the thick skin of buttercup squash, all to go with the goose that was in the roaster crammed full of potato stuffing. Mrs. McMaster pulled out the fruitcakes we'd made, and doused them with rum again. We rolled out piecrust and made pies— pumpkin, mince, and apple. "It wouldn't be Christmas without plenty of desserts," said Mrs. McMaster. "We'll put one aside for Firth and Trent." The girls played with their dolls and sucked on ribbon candy. Little George sat on his sled, pretending he was coasting down a big hill, making all sorts of noises.

"Here comes a bump!" he squealed. From all the way in the kitchen we could hear him. I laughed each time I heard him shriek.

∽

"Where's Georgie?" asked Mrs. McMaster just as we were about to put supper on the table. The wind had picked up during the day and we could hear it whistling through the windows.

"He was sitting on his sled earlier," said Sylvie.

"He put his boots on a short time ago," said Martha.

"What if he ran away?" asked Sylvie.

"Oh, fiddlesticks!" said Mrs. McMaster. "I'm sure he's somewhere right here in this house. I won't be made a fool of. Oh, the stories I could tell about children who went missing and ended up hiding right under everyone's nose."

We searched through the rooms, under the beds, and in every cupboard. We even checked in the post office—though it was the forbidden room in the house—but little George was nowhere to be seen.

Mr. McMaster put on his boots and coat. He looked at me and cleared his throat. "Lark, I'd appreciate your help. Mother, you and the girls stay in here in case he comes back."

I didn't hesitate. Bundling up quickly, I hurried outdoors behind Mr. McMaster.

"I'll check the barn," he said. "You can search the dooryard." I trudged through the snow, trying to move as fast as my feet would allow. The snow tightened around my feet. It felt as though gigantic hands were preventing me from moving forward. I pushed myself harder. It would soon be getting dark.

From behind me in the distance, Mrs. McMaster called out desperately in the winter air for little George to come home. I saw what looked like footprints leading toward the edge of the pasture and decided to follow them. I thought of every possible scenario: George falling through the nearby stream; George frozen stiff in a snowbank. I looked out toward the pasture, searching for any signs of him. The trees cast shadows across the snow. Ice crystals sparkled like broken glass. The wind howled. I could no longer see any footprints. The wind had whipped them away to nothing.

CHAPTER THIRTY-ONE

I STOPPED AND LOOKED ALL AROUND. THE BARN WAS A SILENT SILHOUETTE in the distance. The day was dissolving quickly. I was barely able to make out Mr. McMaster coming out of the barn. But I could see he was alone. The snow was deep and fell into my boots as I trudged forward. Hearing a noise, I stopped to listen. The wind whistled in front of me. Tree branches swayed and then creaked. Looking across the white terrain, I called out for little George. There was only the wind to reply. Soon it would be dark. I was so tired I wasn't sure I could continue on. My cheeks went numb from the cold. My hands and feet tingled.

Fear gripped my heart. Would we find young George before the night overtook us? Pulling my coat close, I turned to face the wind. When it finally stilled, I thought I heard a sound. The wind pulled George's name from my lips when I called out. I waited, but heard nothing. Not far from where I stood was a winter beech, its brown leaves shivering in the wind. I scrambled toward it. It was small, barely more than a branch.

"Keep going, Lark...You know you can keep going," came a whisper in the wind. I thought about Papa, his way of encouraging me, and my spirits lifted.

I called out for little George once more. The scream came right from the bottoms of my feet. The wind stilled in perfect cooperation. Hope swirled on the crest of the snow as I waited for a reply.

"Lark? Is that you, Lark? I'm here. Over here!" came a faint voice in the distance.

"Stay where you are, Georgie. Don't move a whisker."

I forced my feet though the drifts of snow. The brook was not far away. It gurgled and bubbled and begged me to hurry. Twilight was settling fast. On the crust of the white snow, I could make out a dark form. "I see you, George. I'm coming. Don't move. I'm coming!"

Knee-deep in the snow, George's sled was hung up on a rock mere inches from the brook.

"What were you doing, running off like that?" I cried as I picked him up out of the snow. I wasn't sure if I should hug the daylights out of him or scold him for scaring the wits out of us all.

"I was on my way to the moon," he sniffed, rubbing his mitten across his nose.

"The moon?"

"I thought I would make it if I took my sled...But I think you're right, Lark. It would be much faster to go by horse."

"George McMaster!" I exclaimed. "What am I going to do with you?"

"Can you take me home, Lark? It's getting too dark to see now and my feet are cold."

Through the wind and dim light, Mr. McMaster made his way across the field. I waved my arms in the air. "Over here!" I called out. "We're here."

He all but ran to where we were. I wondered, as he hurried toward us, what punishment he would bestow upon little George. Huffing and puffing like a steam engine coming across the crest of the snow, Mr. McMaster was soon upon us. For a few moments he said nothing, although I was certain relief spread across his face when he saw little George standing in the snow.

"Come on up," he said, "It's getting dark." He picked little George up and carried him home on his shoulders. Young George was beaming brighter than a ray of moonlight, sitting up there so high in the air. I followed behind, dragging the sled.

"Look at me, Lark! I can almost touch the moon," Georgie called down to me. He was stretching his arms up high in the air. The moon was now visible and appeared huge on the horizon, big and round and bright, like a pumpkin. Little George poked his father on top of the head. Mr. McMaster looked up at him. "Papa," he said, "don't ever go to the moon without a horse, or you'll never make it."

"Enough of your nonsense, young man," said Mr. McMaster, and little George became quiet. My heart dropped. Why had I dared to think things would change?

We were met in the doorway by the warm smells of Christmas and a band of anxious people, their faces filled with relief.

"You had us worried near to death," scolded Mrs. McMaster as she pulled little George's arms out of his coat sleeves. "We turned this place upside down looking for you." Standing in the doorway, she shook the snow from his jacket. "Shame on you," she continued.

"Yes, Georgie," chimed in Sylvie. "Shame."

Martha took his hat and mitts. "You know better than to run off like that," she added. Little George scowled and kicked the boots from his feet. He looked as though he was about to cry, with everyone chiding him the moment he got back.

"What's this?" asked Sylvie pulling something from little George's coat pocket. Little George rushed over and grabbed it from her.

"It's for Lark," he said, turning toward me. "I found them by the brook, but then I got stuck."

"Dead leaves!" exclaimed Mrs. McMaster. "What could you be thinking? Who would want dead leaves?"

"Winter beech," I corrected, taking the handful of dried leaves from his tiny hand. Mrs. McMaster and the girls laughed, but stopped suddenly when I added, "And the perfect Christmas gift. Thank you, Georgie." I was smiling so big I thought my jaw might stay stuck. Reaching out, I tousled his hair and he gave me a hug.

Mr. McMaster cleared his throat. "That's enough from all of you. George is cold and hungry. We can discuss this later. At this rate it'll be next Christmas before we have anything to eat. Won't it, Georgie?" He walked over to little George and picked him up. For a brief moment he held him close; then he sat him in his chair at the table. I'm not sure who was more surprised—us or little George. Standing there with our mouths dropped open, we hardly knew what to do. A vague smile spread across Mr. McMaster's face as he realized that he had been caught in an awkward moment.

"How's that goose doing?" he quickly asked.

I hurried to help Mrs. McMaster get supper on the table. Little George sat in his chair grinning like he was never going to stop. The room fill up with excitement as our Christmas took on a special meaning. I knew right then that little George had finally found his story to tell.

On my way past the parlour that evening, I looked in to see little George sitting on his father's lap. Mr. McMaster was holding the last tree ornament his wife had begun making and was talking to little George. He smiled at little George and carefully placed the ornament in his open palm.

"What a sight that is," whispered Mrs. McMaster, now standing behind me.

"Indeed, Mrs. McMaster...indeed it is."

"This place has certainly changed," said Brock Cameron many months later. He was sitting at the kitchen table, spreading a piece of bread with molasses. It was the end of August, and little George had just headed off to school that morning with his sisters. He looked all grown up, or so his father told him, much to little George's pleasure. Mr. McMaster had stood in the doorway watching his children walk down the long, narrow driveway toward the main road. "Trent and Firth can take the team out," he'd said. "I'll catch up with them later. I promised Georgie I'd wave him goodbye on his very first day."

"Changed?" I poured Brock a cup of tea, pretending not to know what he was talking about.

He took a sip of tea. "I believe it has something to do with the hired girl who came here to work a year ago," he added with a smile. "What do you think?"

"I think life is always changing, Brock Cameron." I thought back to all the changes that had come about in my life this past year.

"I believe you're right, missy," Brock said. "I knew, that first morning when I brought you to the big front door, something in this house was about to change."

ACKNOWLEDGEMENTS

THE CHARACTER OF LARK HARNISH WAS INSPIRED BY MY GOOD FRIEND and neighbour Oran Veinot, who had a habit of speaking her mind and loved nothing more than to share her stories with others. Her sense of humour and determination inspired so many of us over the years. I began writing Lark's story many years ago and would have loved to have shared this book with Oran, but that wasn't meant to be. My gratitude always for her friendship and the stories she passed on to the people in her life.

Thanks to my family and friends for your unwavering support and for actually reading the stories I write. Thanks to my kids for allowing me to bounce ideas around with them. We don't always accomplish a great deal, but we have fun trying.

My thanks to cousins Marlene and Calvin for answering some of my obscure farming questions while I was working on the edits for this book.

Much appreciation to my friends Bonnie and Judi for your hard work in putting together some amazing book launches over the years; every author should be so lucky. And Bonnie, my "phone friend," please know how good it is to hear your voice on the other end of the phone. Thanks to Gail for keeping my spirits up during some challenging times. I have enjoyed your beautiful cards and positive messages.

Thanks to my editor, Penelope Jackson, for bringing me through the edits of my last six books. Despite my times of uncertainty, your faith in my writing ability remains constant.

My continued gratitude to the team at Nimbus Publishing and Vagrant Press and to Whitney Moran for accepting Lark's story for publication; this book has been a very long time coming, but we finally made it.

Lastly, to all the readers out there who continue to support me, you give my work meaning and purpose.

Angela Haggerty

LAURA BEST has had over forty short stories published in literary magazines and anthologies. Her first young adult novel, *Bitter, Sweet*, was shortlisted for the Geoffrey Bilson Award for Historical Fiction for Young People. Her middle grade novel *Flying with a Broken Wing* was named one of Bank Street College of Education's Best Books of 2015, and its follow-up, *Cammie Takes Flight*, was nominated for the 2018 Silver Birch Award. She published a prequel to the Cammie series, *The Family Way*, in Spring 2021, followed by the standalone historical middle-grade novel *A Sure Cure for Witchcraft*, in Fall 2021. Her first novel for adults, *Good Mothers Don't*, was published in 2020. She lives in East Dalhousie, Nova Scotia, with her husband, Brian. Visit lauraabest.wordpress.com.